WARRIOR'S RESOLVE

IRON HORSE LEGACY BOOK #5

ELLE JAMES

TWISTED PAGE INC

WARRIOR'S RESOLVE

IRON HORSE LEGACY BOOK #5

New York Times & USA Today
Bestselling Author

ELLE JAMES

AUTHOR'S NOTE

Enjoy other books by Elle James

Iron Horse Legacy
Soldier's Duty (#1)
Ranger's Baby (#2)
Marine's Promise (#3)
SEAL's Vow (#4)
Warrior's Resolve (#5)

Visit ellejames.com for more titles and release dates
For hot cowboys, visit her alter ego Myla Jackson at
mylajackson.com
and join Elle James's Newsletter at
https://ellejames.com/contact/

CHAPTER 1

"HAVE the Brotherhood Protectors dug any deeper into the corporation that paid Otis Ferguson to torture Mr. McKinnon?" Parker Bailey walked with Angus, the oldest McKinnon son, to the barn to check on the horses and throw them some hay.

"Not yet. Some corporations bury ownership so deep, it takes a court subpoena or extremely effective hacking skills to extract the information," Angus said. "Hank Patterson has Swede working on it. If anyone can hack into that corporation's database, he can. Problem is, it takes time. We're not sure how much time my father has. His kidnappers have to be getting desperate by now."

Parker frowned. "But they'll keep him alive if they think he knows where the money is, right?"

"That's what we're banking on," Angus said. "We know now that they tortured him, and he didn't reveal the location. His kidnappers will have to do something else to make him give up that data."

"Knowing how stubborn Mr. McKinnon can be, the only way they'll get him to tell is if they threaten something or someone he cares about." Parker shook his head. "He cares most about his family. You know it's only a matter of time before they target one of you. Are you ready, should that situation arise?"

Angus shook his head. "We all know to keep on the lookout for trouble. But we can't hole up and hide. We have a ranch to run, and we need to keep looking for my father."

"At the very least, you need to put your foot down with Molly. She's not following the buddy rule. You never know who'll be out there, waiting for an opportunity to snatch one of you and use you to make your father talk."

"Why don't you bring it up at dinner?" Angus said.

"I think it would be better coming from you. Your siblings look up to and respect you."

Angus grinned. "And you don't want to have to tell Molly she can't just ride out anytime she feels like it. Alone."

Parker's lips pressed into a tight line. "She doesn't listen to me. The woman would just as soon spit on me as follow any of my advice."

With a chuckle, Angus nodded. "You seem to get sideways with her a lot. Why do you suppose that is?"

"Beats the heck out of me. I try to stay clear of

her. She's a loose cannon and has a temper that gives her a short fuse."

"That's our Molly. I think my father spoiled her, being the youngest and the only girl." Angus clapped a hand on Parker's shoulder. "I would have thought as a former Air Force pararescue PJ, you wouldn't be afraid of anything."

Parker bristled. "I'm not afraid of Molly."

"No?" Angus tilted his head. "Hell, I am, most of the time. You're right. She has a temper. And when she thinks she's right, she's like a dog with a bone. She won't let it go."

"That's the truth." Parker liked that about her. She didn't back down one bit. Raised with four older brothers, she'd no doubt grown up having to defend herself against their taunts and teasing.

Angus reached the barn first and opened the door, holding it for Parker to go in first.

Once inside, Angus closed the door and looked around. "I'll get the hay. You can get the water."

"Deal," Parker said and went to the side of the barn with the hose connected to a spigot. He turned on the water and uncoiled the hose to reach across the barn to the farthest stall where Rusty, Molly's sorrel gelding, resided. Only the gelding wasn't in his stall.

Parker swore, hurried to the barn door and looked out into the nearby pasture for Rusty. When he didn't spot the horse, he ducked into the tack room and swore again.

Parker's pulse kicked up a couple notches. "When was the last time you saw Molly?" he asked Angus as he exited the tack room.

"This morning." Angus tossed hay into a stall and brushed the loose straw and dust off his hands. "Why?"

"Her horse is gone."

"She was talking about repairing that fence in the southeast pasture. Several strands were cut, and some of the cattle got through."

Parker's pulse ratcheted up, and he swore. "And I specifically told her I'd do it later today. Do you know if she at least took one of your brothers with her?"

Angus shook his head. "No. If I recall, Colin and Duncan went to town for feed and groceries. Bastian went with Jenna to look at a property."

"Which means Molly is out on the ranch by herself. And she's been out most of the day." Parker's chest tightened. "Doesn't she realize she's a prime target?"

Angus's lips twisted. "She's always been hard-headed. You can't tell her anything."

"I'll saddle up and go look for her."

"I will, too," Angus said. "There were a couple of places where the fence needed mending. We can split up and check both."

Parker led Franco, his piebald gelding, out of his stall and tied him to a metal loop on a post. Then he hurried to the tack room and grabbed a saddle, blanket and bridle.

Angus saddled Jack, the black gelding he preferred to ride during his visits home from active duty.

When they were ready, Angus opened the pasture fence and waited for Parker and Franco to pass through. He led his horse through and closed the gate, mounted and tipped his head to the north. "I'll take the northwest corner and work my way around to the south along the fence line."

"And I'll start on the southeast corner and work my way around to the north," Parker said. "Whoever finds her first should fire off a round so the other won't keep looking."

Angus nodded, nudged his horse's flanks with his heels and galloped across the pasture heading north.

Parker worried that his boss's daughter had been out all day long with no backup. The sun had already sunk low on the horizon. It wouldn't be long before it dropped below the peaks of the Crazy Mountains.

Molly should've been back at the ranch house by now. The nights were cold. Wolves and bears came out in the evening. Not only could she be a target for the people who'd kidnapped her father, she'd be hunted by the wild animals native to the Montana countryside.

His grip tightened on the reins as he urged the horse to a gallop and leaned into wind. His need to find her grew with each passing mile. Heart racing, he remembered another time he'd been sent in to rescue a Black Hawk helicopter pilot.

The mission had gone south fast. Not only did he get injured, he hadn't been able to rescue the pilot before he'd been shot and killed. The man had had a wife and two small children. Parker had never forgiven himself for being too late to save him.

His job as a member of the US Air Force's Pararescue team had been to medically treat and rescue military personnel in combat or humanitarian environments.

On that last mission, he'd failed, and his injury had caused him to be medically retired from service.

Thankfully, James McKinnon had seen something in him that Parker had thought he'd lost, and hired him on the spot.

He'd known Molly for all of the five years he'd worked at the Iron Horse Ranch. When he'd first come, she'd been a thorn in his side, always hanging around, giving him advice on how they did things there. He'd soon learned she was as smart as a whip and one of the best ranchers he'd ever known.

Her family didn't give her enough credit for all she did and all she knew about caring for the animals her family owned. So many times, because she was a woman, they didn't think she was fully capable of ranching.

While her brothers had all gone off to the military, following in their father's footsteps, Molly had stayed on Iron Horse Ranch and had learned everything there was to know about ranching, from calving, branding and worming to managing the books. She'd even brought the ranch's banking and bookkeeping into the twenty-first century by transferring the data from old manual ledgers to computer software. She'd had to drag her father along, kicking and screaming, metaphorically speaking.

As much as Parker wanted to dislike the boss's daughter, he had great respect for her abilities. She was the kind of woman he could see himself with—smart, physically strong and beautiful.

If only she wasn't the boss's daughter.

When Parker had signed on with James McKinnon as his foreman five years ago, Molly had just graduated college with an accounting degree and a minor in animal husbandry. The fresh-faced college grad came home and dove into ranching with a passion. She was beautiful, young and a threat to Parker's focus. He'd promised himself he wouldn't get involved.

To keep his promise to himself, he treated Molly like a pesky kid sister, irritating the fire out of her every chance he got.

A smile briefly tugged at the corners of his lips as

he rode across the pasture toward the southeastern border of the massive Montana ranch, tucked into the foothills of the Crazy Mountains.

He might be overreacting about the danger Molly could be in, but he'd rather be safe than have her kidnapped to force James McKinnon into telling his abductors anything.

He urged his horse to go faster.

MOLLY MCKINNON HAMMERED horseshoe-shaped nails into a wooden fence post, securing the strand of barbed wire she'd just stretched over one hundred feet. It was the last strand. Once she released the pressure from the come-along and packed away her tools, she'd head home.

She should have been home hours ago, but she'd spent much of her day herding the Iron Horse cattle back inside the confines of the ranch's fence. Once they were back on the right side, Molly had gone to work stretching the barbed wire that had been cut and patching it where it no longer fit.

Hot, sweaty and way past hungry, she brushed hair out of her face that had slipped from her ponytail. She straightened, working the kinks out of her back, and glanced at the clear blue Montana sky. The sun was just touching the mountain peaks. It wouldn't be much longer before the rays dipped below the ridges and sank below the other side.

Darkness came early to the mountain valleys. She'd need to head back to the ranch house soon or be caught out after dark. Not that she was afraid of the dark. Her concern was more a matter of being respectful of what lurked in the shadows. Wolves and bears moved around at night. She had her rifle in the holster on her saddle, if she needed to defend herself from four-legged animals, as well as the two-legged kind.

She'd just packed the hammer and bag of nails in her saddlebag and tied the come-along to the back of the saddle. With her foot in the stirrup, about to pull herself up onto her horse Rusty, she heard the roar of engines coming from the nearby woods.

Rusty's ears flattened, and he reared, whinnying sharply. Caught with only one foot in the stirrup, Molly fell backward, landing so hard on her back that all the air left her lungs in a whoosh.

Before she could recover, Rusty turned and raced away...with her rifle.

Two ATVs leaped out of the tree line and sped straight for her.

Molly sucked in a breath, shot to her feet and ran. She aimed for a copse of trees, hoping to duck in and hide before the ATV riders reached her.

Running as fast as she could in her cowboy boots, she could hear the four-wheelers behind her, catching up.

A glance over her shoulder made her yelp and run faster.

One of the men slowed, raised his right hand with a gun in it and fired.

Something stung the back of Molly's neck. It didn't feel like a bullet. She reached back and touched something that felt like a dart. She plucked it out of her skin, realizing it was either a poison dart or one laced with a drug to make her...sleepy.

Molly stumbled, her head getting heavy, her feet hard to lift from the ground.

The four-wheelers circled her, forcing her to stop running. It seemed like everywhere she turned an ATV blocked her path. The more she spun, the dizzier she became.

Just when she thought she might fall, a shot rang out from a distance.

One of the men on the ATVs jerked, his hand leaving the handlebar, his ATV veering out of the tight circle he'd been holding around Molly.

Molly took that moment to lunge through the gap. She staggered, ran and fell to her knees.

Another shot rang out.

The men on the ATVs turned and raced for the woods.

In the gathering dusk, a horseback rider charged toward Molly.

She pushed to her feet and ran, fear making her heart pound hard in her chest. Her breathing ragged, she fought to fill her lungs and keep moving, though every step was like walking through a thick mire of mud.

Molly wanted to lie down on the ground and sleep.

"Molly!" a familiar voice shouted. "Take my hand."

She looked up into a familiar face. "Parker? What are you doing here?" she asked, though her words slurred, and her vision blurred.

"Take my hand, dammit!" he shouted.

That's when she noticed he held out a hand.

Automatically, she placed hers in his.

"Put your foot in the stirrup. Hurry!"

"Why are you yelling at me?" she grumbled, while trying to place the toe of her boot into the empty stirrup, but she couldn't quite reach it.

His hand wrapped tightly around hers. "Focus, Molly. They're coming back. We don't have time to miss."

She narrowed her eyes and concentrated on placing her foot into the stirrup. Once it was there, she was yanked up onto the saddle in front of Parker, landing hard in his lap.

Finally, she could relax and stop running. Molly melted into his arms and lay her cheek against his shoulder.

Parker wrapped an arm around her. "Hold onto the saddle horn. It's going to be a rough ride."

With one hand on the horn and the other encircling Parker's waist, she held on as best her fuzzy mind could allow.

The horse leaped forward and broke into a gallop.

"Rusty," she said.

"Is on his way back to the barn. I passed him on my way here."

"Can't...stay...awake," Molly said, though her tongue felt like it was swollen and uncooperative.

"You have to," Parker urged. "We're being followed. And they have guns."

"I know," she said. "Shot me...dart."

Parker swore and reined the horse toward a line of trees. Hooves pounding in the ground felt like they were pounding into her head and her entire body. She wanted the world to stop and let her just sleep. *But no.*

Parker kept up the pace.

The roar of four-wheeler engines sounded behind them, moving closer.

When they reached the trees, Parker didn't slow. Several times he ducked, pushing her head down to avoid a low hanging branch.

Still, the ATVs drew nearer.

"Hold on tight," Parker urged.

He aimed the horse toward a steep embankment that dropped down sharply into a narrow valley.

The horse balked, and then stepped over the edge, slipping and sliding downward, loose gravel and dirt cascading down with them.

Molly clung to Parker as he swayed in the saddle, guiding the horse on a path barely wide enough for the horse's hooves. Certainly not wide enough for a four-wheeler.

When they reached the bottom, the horse stretched his legs and raced across a meadow and into the shelter of yet more trees.

The engine noise faded behind them but continued to follow at a distance.

Molly glanced up at the trail they'd left. Two men on ATVs drove parallel to them from above, tracking them as they moved through the valley.

Franco emerged into a wide-open pasture, and Parker gave his piebald gelding his head.

The horse flew across the field, heading for the barn.

Another horseback rider appeared from the north and ran beside them.

Parker jerked his head toward their rear and shouted to the other rider. "Trouble!"

As the other rider turned, the setting sun illuminated his face, and Molly finally recognized the man as her oldest brother.

Angus slowed his horse and drew his rifle out of the scabbard beside his knee. He aimed it in the direction of the hills and the sound of the ATVs.

Molly looked over Parker's shoulder, wanting to tell her brother to be careful.

The four-wheelers burst from a trail, heading toward her brother.

Shots rang out.

The ATVs spun and headed back into the trees.

Angus remained where he was for a few moments longer, his weapon raised and ready.

When the ATVs didn't reappear, he turned his horse and raced after Parker and Molly.

Molly sighed and leaned into Parker.

He smelled of aftershave and leather.

She liked that. No fancy cologne, just Parker, the Montana range and a setting sun. What more could a girl want?

She closed her eyes, the rocking, pounding motion of the horse making it harder and harder for her to stay awake.

Finally, they arrived at the gate to the barnyard.

Her mother rushed forward and opened the gate, her horse beside her. "What happened?" she cried out. "When Rusty came back without Molly, I was worried. I was about to come out looking for her."

"I'm not sure what's wrong with her," Parker said. "She can barely hold her head up."

"Sleepy," Molly murmured.

Angus rode through the gate behind them, leaped down from his horse and reached up to catch Molly as she slipped out of Parker's arms. He let her feet touch the ground, then slung one of her arms around his shoulder and wrapped an arm around her waist.

"Hey, bro," she slurred. "Just put me down here. I need a nap."

"Drugged," he said, his lips forming a thin line.

Parker dropped to the ground beside Angus. "I'll take her up to the house."

Molly's legs gave out. "Don't know why nothing's working. Probably because I'm sleepy."

Parker scooped her up into his arms. "I'll get her to her room, if you can take care of the horses."

Angus frowned. "The horses can wait. I want to know what they did to her."

"I'll call the doctor," Molly's mom said and raced ahead of them toward the house.

Molly closed her eyes for a second. When she opened them again, Parker was laying her on the couch and pulling off her boots.

"Need to take care of Rusty," she said, though her words came out as no more than a whisper. When she tried to sit up, her body didn't respond. She lay like a limp rag doll, unable to move even a finger.

"Your brothers will take care of your horse. Just lie still. The doctor's on his way."

"Don't need a doctor," she said. "Just need a nap." Again, she closed her eyes. "Anyone ever tell you that you smell good?"

Parker's chuckle warmed what was cold inside her and made her relax. "Why do you hate me?" she whispered.

"I don't hate you," he said quietly.

"Sure act like it," she groused.

"Shhh. You're going to be all right," he said, as if soothing a child.

"Because of you." Her eyelids were so heavy now she couldn't open them. Molly embraced the darkness and let her mind and body slip away. Later, she'd worry about those men who'd shot her and why Parker was all of a sudden being nice to her.

CHAPTER 2

PARKER STAYED by Molly's side, holding one hand while her mother held the other. She was out cold but breathing regularly. Still, the fact she was out cold worried him. What drug had they shot into her? The only way to tell would be to take a blood sample and have it analyzed.

When the doctor arrived, he and Molly's mother shooed Parker away. He found her brothers in Mr. McKinnon's study.

"What the hell happened out there?" Angus asked, as soon as Parker walked through the door. "One minute, I'm riding the fences, the next I hear multiple gunshots."

"Seriously, what the hell?" Bastian, the youngest brother, and closest to Molly, stood with his arms crossed over his chest.

"When we discovered your sister's horse missing, Angus and I went out looking for her," Parker said.

"I went north. Parker headed south." Angus nodded for Parker to continue.

"I was almost to the southeast corner of the farthest pasture when I heard engines. That's when Molly's horse raced past me...without Molly."

The brothers' eyebrows dipped.

Parker continued. "When I broke through a line of trees, two ATVs were circling Molly. She seemed drunk, staggering and falling down. I fired a round at the men on the ATVs. Winged one of them, and he veered off. Molly made a dash for it. I fired again, and the other rider followed the injured one into the trees—I guess to regroup. It gave me time to pick up Molly and ride out. Then they followed us. We took a narrow game trail down a ravine and out into the pasture." He tipped his head toward Angus. "Thankfully, Angus was there to provide cover while I got Molly back to the house."

Silence followed as all four brothers stood frowning and shaking their heads.

"So, it begins," Duncan said, breaking the silence.

Colin heaved a sigh. "Since they can't get Dad to tell them what he knows, they're going to target us."

Bastian nodded. "Looks like they're wanting to take one of us captive."

"What the hell was Molly doing out there alone, anyway?" Colin demanded. "We talked about this."

"You know your sister," Parker said. "She's stubborn. Probably thought she was well armed and capable of taking care of herself."

"As far as this entire family is concerned, none of us are capable of taking care of ourselves alone," Angus said. "Do you know what I mean?"

His brothers nodded.

Angus stared hard at his brothers. "No one leaves this house without backup."

"*Armed* backup," Parker added.

"Even just going to town?" Colin asked.

"Even then," Angus confirmed.

"That should include going out to the barn, as well," Parker said.

"And no one should be left alone in the house," Angus said. "Mom might think she's safe here, but I'm not so sure."

"I know where I'll be," Duncan said.

Angus nodded. "With Fiona and Caity. That's a given. Your daughter will be a target as much as the rest of us. At least, they're living here now."

"I wouldn't put it past whoever's responsible for Dad's kidnapping to target our women to get to us," Colin said.

"It's a good thing most of the ladies live on the ranch now," Bastian noted.

Angus frowned. "I'd move Bree here, but she has her own place to run." Angus paused. "As much as I want her here, I'll have to go to her ranch to protect her."

Bastian's lips twisted. "If I know Jenna, she won't quit showing properties. I'll be escorting her around during the day. The good thing about looking at properties is we get around the area. We'll keep our eyes peeled for any signs of Dad."

"With Duncan at the house, Angus with Bree, and Bastian out with Jenna, that leaves Colin, Molly and Parker to deal with the ranch." Angus frowned. "Do we need to hire some of Hank Patterson's Brotherhood Protectors to provide another layer of security?"

"It wouldn't hurt," Duncan said. "If we hire them to secure the house, we can be backup for each other out on the ranch."

"I'm not even sure the buddy system will be enough." Parker's eyes narrowed. "They only sent out two people to secure Molly. And it would have worked if I hadn't come along."

"They drugged her. Likely darted her." Angus's brow dipped low.

"They must have known she'd fight back," Bastian said. "Hard. Like only our little sister would."

Parker shook his head. "By the time I got to her, she was as effective as a limp noodle." His hands clenched into fists. "They would've taken her and tortured her to persuade your father to give them the location of that money."

"I hope this incident convinces Molly never to leave the house without backup," Duncan said.

Bastian snorted. "Since when has Molly ever listened to one of us?"

"Good point." Angus turned to Parker. "Since the rest of us are going to be worrying about our women, and Duncan will be here with Mother, that leaves you to look out for Molly. She won't listen to us, because we're only her pesky older brothers. She might listen to you."

Parker scowled. "Your sister doesn't listen to anyone."

"Then it'll be up to you to keep up with her," Angus said.

"Stick to her like a fly on flypaper," Colin said.

"Like gum on your shoe," offered Bastian.

"Like stink on—" Duncan started.

Parker held up a hand. "I get the idea. The trouble is, Molly has a mind of her own. I never know when she's going to up and ride out to fix fences or chase down a horse with a lame foot or drive into town for supplies."

Angus rubbed a hand through his hair. "As evidenced by her disappearance today."

"Well, after this afternoon's attack, maybe she'll be more open to the buddy system." Bastian clapped a hand on Parker's shoulder. "Since you saved her ass today, she owes you."

"The problem is that the men holding Dad are

getting desperate." Angus paced across the floor. "We have to keep a closer eye on Mom and Molly."

Duncan nodded. "Dad's captors have to know that those are the two family members to go after. If our father sees either one of them in trouble, he'll tell them anything they want to hear or die trying to save his girls."

Parker had been around long enough to know James McKinnon loved his family. The Marine in him made him seem taciturn, but he fiercely loved his wife, sons and daughter.

"Parker," Angus said with a frown, "living out in the foreman's house isn't going to work. You'll have to move into the big house. It's the only way you'll know when Molly is coming or going."

Parker held up his hands. "I don't see a need to move into the house. With everyone else sleeping here at night, there should be no problem keeping up with Molly's comings and goings. You just have to let me know when she exits the house."

Bastian frowned. "It's too easy to lose track of her. It's better knowing one person is solely responsible for Molly's whereabouts."

"I'll also talk to Hank Patterson," Angus said. "Maybe they have some tracking devices we can put on all of the ladies. That way, if one of them is misplaced, we can find them."

"Good idea," Colin said. "And the sooner the better."

"Parker, you can have my room, since I'll be staying with Bree at her ranch," Angus said. "It works out well because my room is next to Molly's. You'll know when she's moving about and can head her off at the pass before she leaves the house."

"I was paid to work with horses and cattle, not to babysit the boss's daughter," Parker muttered.

"You know, we all think of you as family," Duncan said. "But if it bothers you, think of it as preserving your job. If something happened to Molly or our mother, my father would be devastated. He'd sell this place."

Bastian shook his head. "No, he'd burn it to the ground and walk away. He loves our mother and sister that much."

"So," Colin concluded, "if you want to keep working at Iron Horse Ranch, you need to stay on top of Molly." He frowned. "Figuratively speaking."

Duncan's eyebrows sank. "And remember, she is our sister. Don't break her heart or anything like that. We love her, even if she is a pain in the ass."

Parker snorted. "If you love her so much, why doesn't one of you take on the responsibility of keeping track of her?"

"Remember the part about her being a pain in our ass?" Bastian chuckled. "And that she doesn't listen to a word we say?"

Parker smirked. "And you think she'll listen to me?"

"Probably not, but you have more patience with her than we do," Angus said. "And you've both been working the ranch. It makes sense you'd continue doing that together."

Parker's jaw tightened. "You realize the ranch is a big place. We didn't exactly work *together*." Hell, he'd spent the past five years avoiding her, choosing to work wherever she was not. The woman was difficult, opinionated...and too damned sexy for his peace of mind.

"So, now you just do your things...together," Bastian said. "What could be so hard about that?"

You have no idea.

Parker might as well have been talking to a brick wall. The McKinnon brothers had voted him off the island. He was the one stuck babysitting their little sister.

If he was honest with himself, he'd rather it be him, anyway. The image of those men on ATVs circling Molly had scared at least a year off his life. He couldn't imagine doing that again. At the same time, he couldn't imagine anyone else looking after her. No one had noticed she'd been gone all day.

Molly was like that. If she saw something that needed doing, she did it. She didn't wait around for someone to help or offer to do it for her. No. She got out her gloves, hammer and come-along and went to work.

He admired that about her. At the same time, he

found her aggravating and impetuous. Somehow, he had to get it through her thick head that she had to have someone as backup. For just such an incident as what had happened that night. Before, attacks on the family had been speculation. After the ATV riders had shot her with a sedative and corralled her on the prairie, Parker and everyone else on Iron Horse Ranch were convinced they were being targeted in order to force their father to tell his captors where the money was hidden.

Why did James McKinnon have to be the last man to see the convict who'd escaped prison and come back to Eagle Rock and the Crazy Mountains of Montana to find the loot he'd stolen from an armored truck robbery?

The manhunt to find the convict hadn't gone well at all. The convict had been shot, James McKinnon had been abducted and the money the convict had stolen remained hidden.

Now, Parker was responsible for the life of the patriarch's daughter.

He drew in a deep breath and let it out slowly. Better him than someone else. At the very least, he'd keep a tight rein on her until they recovered Mr. McKinnon and brought to justice the men who'd captured him.

~

MOLLY WOKE the next morning with a headache, a bruise on the back of her neck and feeling like she hadn't had a bath in a week. She felt awful but refused to remain in bed. Mostly, she was mad. Mad that she'd been caught unprepared. Mad that her father's captors had almost caught their prize, and would have, if Parker Bailey hadn't shown up when he had. Finally, she was mad that it had been Parker who'd come to her rescue.

The man drove her insane. When her father had hired him to be foreman of the ranch, Molly had been disappointed that her father hadn't thought she was fully capable of the job. She'd been ranching since the day she was born.

During high school, Parker had worked summers on a ranch in Wyoming but had joined the Air Force as soon as he'd graduated.

Molly had years more experience than Parker and had resented the fact he'd been put in charge over her.

Plus, from the day he'd come to work at Iron Horse Ranch, he'd teased her relentlessly, whenever they were in the same workspace, or avoided her altogether.

What made her even madder was that Parker had proven he was good at ranching. Over the past five years, he'd worked hard, made suggestions for improving everything from fencing to cattle breeding and horse training. When he wasn't out working, he was reading, researching best practices and learning.

Again, she couldn't find fault in that, though she wanted to.

The funny thing about Parker was he never dated. Molly had begun to wonder about his past. Had some woman hurt him so badly he wasn't willing to jump back into the dating scene? Five years was a long time for a man to go without a woman in his life. Unless he was seeing someone on his time off. Once a month, he took a weekend off and left the ranch, to where, Molly didn't know. Was he seeing someone?

The thought of Parker seeing someone didn't sit right in Molly's gut. After five years on the ranch, he was a fixture. A swarthy, sexy-when-he-removed-his-shirt fixture. Imagining another woman running her hands over his muscular physique made Molly's insides churn.

Gathering clean clothes, she wrapped a bathrobe around her body and hurried across the hallway to the bathroom. A hot shower was what she needed to clean away the dirt from working and being run into the ground by the men on ATVs yesterday.

She wasn't sure who'd carried her to her room the night before. Someone had to have brought her up because she couldn't remember climbing the stairs to get there. Her mother must have stripped her clothes off. At least, she hoped that was how her clothing had been changed. Her body heated at the thought of Parker doing the job.

Molly shook her head. No, her mother would have done that.

After a hot shower, where she scrubbed every inch of her body, she dried and stood naked in front of the mirror and thanked her lucky stars she only had a few cuts and bruises. If those assholes had gotten hold of her, she'd have been in a lot worse shape.

On the other hand, they might have taken her to her father. If that had happened, she might have come up with a plan to free him.

She pinched the bridge of her nose to try to stem her headache. Whatever they'd given her had been strong enough to make her dizzy, disoriented and unable to defend herself. How would she have helped her father if they'd kept her drugged like that?

Dressing in clean jeans and a long-sleeved flannel shirt, she brushed her wet hair back and plaited it into a French braid, securing it with an elastic band.

She brushed her teeth and made a face at herself in the mirror.

Parker was probably seeing another woman. Why would he look at someone like Molly McKinnon who didn't wear makeup or comb her hair half the time?

Not that she was one to fish for compliments or attention. She had always considered herself one of the ranch hands, one of the boys. Like her brothers.

Only she'd opted not to join the military and leave Iron Horse Ranch.

Since when did she care what she looked like?

Never.

Molly yanked open the door and charged across the hallway to her room, shoved her feet into her boots, walked out her door and hit a solid wall.

"What the hell?" she exclaimed and stared up at what, at first, she thought was her brother Angus.

When her gaze scraped across his face, her cheeks heated. "Oh. It's you."

Parker Bailey's mouth quirked up at one corner. "Don't sound so excited. I might take it wrong."

Her brow dipped. "I didn't expect you to be in this hallway." Her frown deepened. "What are you doing up here?"

"I've taken over your brother's bedroom for the near future."

"What?" Her eyes rounded. "What do you mean you've taken over my brother's room? Where's Angus?"

"He'll be staying over at Bree Lansing's ranch until we get your father back."

Molly crossed her arms over her chest. "That explains why Angus isn't in his room, but it doesn't explain why you've moved in."

Parker snorted. "I drew the short straw."

What the heck was he talking about? "The short straw for what?"

"With the entire family now at risk, you and your mother especially, your brothers will be tied up keeping track of their women. Duncan will be hanging out here at the house with Fiona, Caity and your mother. Bastian will be escorting Jenna around the county as she does her real estate thing. Colin will be sticking close to Emily, and that leaves you." Parker shrugged. "So, you see, I drew the short straw." He gave her a tight smile. "I'm stuck with you." He shrugged. "Or you could look at it as you're stuck with me. I don't care how you view this situation as long as you don't give me a hard time. I have work to do on this ranch. I'd appreciate it if you'd cooperate and stay within ten feet of me at all times."

Molly gasped, choked on her own tongue and then squeaked, "Stay close to you?"

Parker nodded. "I've been assigned as your babysitter. No wait, I wasn't supposed to call it that. I've been assigned as your backup buddy. Like it or not, I'll be with you every day from sunup to sundown, until your father comes home."

The shower that had calmed her and made her feel better and more in control of herself, wasn't doing anything for her now.

"You're my *babysitter*?" Molly said, her voice rising. "I'm twenty-eight years old. I don't need a babysitter. I'm perfectly capable of taking care of myself."

"Like you did last night?" Parker challenged.

"I was making my escape…" she sputtered.

"Not until I shot one of them," Parker said. "They drugged you. It was only a matter of seconds before they grabbed you and took you to who knows where to do who knows what."

With a hand to the back of her neck, Molly lifted her chin high as she stared at Parker. "I was about to make my move when you showed up. I could've gotten away."

"Drugged?" Parker shook his head. "I have no doubt you could've fought your way free—if you'd been in your right mind." He snorted. "As it was, you could barely stand on your own feet."

He was right, and that fact made Molly even madder. She stopped short of stomping her foot. "I don't need a babysitter."

"There's no one else to back you up. I'm afraid you're stuck with me."

"I can hang out with Colin and Emily," Molly said. "Or go help Jenna and Bastian with real estate. You have enough to do without following me around."

"Yeah, and as soon as I leave you for a moment, you'll be out at the barn, feeding animals, or out on the ranch, fixing more fences."

Molly's cheeks heated again. She'd already been thinking about the other hole in the fence she hadn't gotten to yet. "I only have about an hour's work left on another section of fence."

"Fine. I'll help, and we can get it done even faster."

"I don't need you glued to my side. I can do things on my own. I've been working this ranch since the day I could pull on my own boots. I know how to keep an eye out for danger. I don't need help, and I certainly don't need a babysitter. You can go do what you do, and I'll do what I do. I don't need—"

Parker grabbed her arms and pressed his mouth to hers, effectively cutting off her argument.

Shocked, Molly couldn't move, couldn't think past his lips locked with hers. Sweet Jesus, he tasted like mint toothpaste and smelled of an earthy aftershave.

Her fingers curled into his shirt, and her body went limp against his.

At first, his lips were hard against hers, and his fingers were tight on her arms. As the kiss progressed, his hand slid around the back of her neck, and his fingers wrapped around her braid. He tugged gently.

Molly had never had a man tug on her hair like that. Not like a brother pulling her ponytail, but a lover, angling her head to...

She gasped at the sensations he evoked by pulling her hair. As soon as her mouth opened, his tongue slipped past her teeth and caressed hers in a long, slow glide.

Parker's other hand slid around to her back and lower, pressing her firmly against him and the hard ridge beneath the fly of his jeans.

Her breath caught and held. Her blood was like molten lava pushing through her veins...hot, burning and flowing south to her core.

As quickly as he'd started the kiss, he ended it and stepped back, his arms falling to his sides.

Molly blinked several times, a little dizzy again, this time having nothing to do with the drug shot into her veins and everything to do with the man who'd just kissed her senseless.

She raised her fingers to her swollen lips. "Why... did you do that?"

His lips twitched. "It was the only way I could get a word in edgewise."

Like a splash of cold water, full in the face, his words hit her. She raised her hand to slap his cheek.

He caught her wrist in mid-swing. "I apologize if my method was crude, but it worked. Now, listen."

Molly sputtered and would have ripped him apart with words, if she could've gotten any to come out. Anger boiled in her veins. "How dare you," she whispered. "You had no right to do that. If you'd wanted me to shut up, all you had to do was ask. I'm not a complete idiot. I—"

He shook his head as if he were looking at a half-wit. Then he twisted the arm he'd kept from hitting him up behind her back and pulled her close. "I can do it again. And I will, until you're quiet enough to listen." His mouth hovered over hers. "What's it to be?"

For a moment, Molly considered telling him to go to hell. His reasoning was infuriating and chauvinistic. She had every right to speak. "You wouldn't pull this on one of my brothers," she whispered, both afraid he would kiss her again and equally afraid he wouldn't.

"You're right. But then you aren't your brothers." His lips hovered over hers.

Molly found herself leaning toward him, rising up just a little, willing his mouth to cover hers.

"You're not like your brothers because they will listen to reason. You won't."

That urge to kiss him again vanished, replaced by the desire to cut him off at the knees. "I listen. I just choose to ignore your claim of being my babysitter. I prefer to have one of my brothers as my backup."

Parker shook his head. "Not an option. It's been discussed. I was assigned to you."

Her brow dipped low. "We'll see about that. No one make decisions about me when I'm not present."

"You were unconscious after men drugged you and tried to abduct your ass." Parker waved her toward the staircase. "But go ahead. Ask your brothers. It was their idea for me to follow you around and keep you out of trouble, not mine."

"We'll see about that," Molly said and led the way down the stairs. "Angus, Duncan, Colin, Bastian," she called out.

Duncan ducked his head out of the living room

on the first floor. "Shhh. I just got Caity down for a nap. She didn't sleep well last night, and neither did I or Fiona. Mom's in the kitchen. You might find Colin and Emily there."

"Is my little Caity-bug feeling okay?" Molly asked, concerned for her niece. The child had her wrapped around her chubby little finger.

"I think she can sense the tension in the air. We were all worried about you." Duncan glanced back into the living room at the portable playpen they kept there. "I think she knew and was restless all night."

Guilt knotted in Molly's gut. "I'm sorry. I hope she sleeps well, and you and Fiona get some rest."

"Fiona's sleeping in, but I need to be down here with Mom. Colin and Emily are heading to town soon for supplies. Bastian and Jenna left thirty minutes ago to prepare for a house showing Jenna has scheduled."

"Angus?" Molly asked.

"Is at Bree's ranch. He's afraid whoever came after you might come after any one of the members of our family or our significant others. Even Caity could be targeted. It's got us all on edge."

That knot in her belly grew tighter. "I'd hate for anything to happen to Caity, Mom or any one of you," Molly said.

"Same here," Duncan said. "Last night was a real eye-opener and a reminder. We didn't think anything could be as bad as losing Dad to whoever kidnapped him, but the thought of losing any more of our family is unacceptable."

Caity fussed in the living room.

Duncan turned toward her, his brow wrinkling.

"Go, check on her," Molly said. "I'm headed for the kitchen."

"Mom's pretty worn out," Duncan warned her. "It's been a lot for her to process. She was beside herself when they brought you in last night."

Tears welled in her eyes. "Mom doesn't need anything else to go wrong. She's had enough."

Duncan nodded. "Agreed." Caity cried out. "That's my cue." He hurried into the living room to rescue his baby girl from the playpen.

Molly moved toward the kitchen, Parker at her heels. "You don't have to say it," she spoke softly.

"Say what?" Parker responded.

"I told you so," Molly said. "I get it. Everyone is worried, and what happened yesterday didn't help."

Parker didn't respond.

"I shouldn't have gone out on my own. I just didn't think anything could happen to me. Hell, I had a rifle."

"That came back to the barn with your horse and not you," Parker reminded her.

Molly sighed. "Rusty spooked."

"That's why it's good to have someone with you at all times as backup. If I'd been there, they would never have gotten close enough to drug you with a dart."

Molly stopped in the hallway and faced Parker. "God, I hate it when you're right." Her eyes narrowed. "Fine. I'll let you follow me around and be my backup, but I don't have to like it."

"No, you don't. And you don't have to make it difficult. The first time you try to give me the slip, I swear, I'll handcuff you to me and throw away the key. I work for the Iron Horse Ranch. I take my responsibilities seriously. Apparently, you're now one of my responsibilities."

"Fine. I promise not to ditch you." She snorted. "I find it quite ironic that you're the one who always managed to ditch *me* in the past."

"That was then," he said. "The circumstances have changed."

Her brows rose. "So, you admit it? You did ditch me all those times?"

His smile both irritated her and made her heartbeat flutter uncontrollably.

"I don't know what you're talking about," he said and pushed the door open to the kitchen. "Good morning, Mrs. McKinnon," he said, indicating the end to his and Molly's conversation.

Well, hell, she was now stuck with Parker Bailey as her bodyguard and resident shadow. Touching a hand to her still tingling lips, she wondered how working so close to him was going to change their relationship. Already, he'd said more than two words to her, which was more than he'd said every day for the past five years. And he'd kissed her. Not once, but nearly twice! Her breath caught in her lungs. Why did the man have such an effect on her?

Who knew? Maybe something good could come of being drugged and almost kidnapped.

CHAPTER 3

PARKER COULD HAVE KICKED himself from here to tomorrow. What had come over him to break all his self-imposed rules and kiss the boss's daughter?

All the years he'd kept his distance, avoiding her whenever possible and remaining strictly hands off, had flown out the window with that first kiss.

And then to have almost kissed her a second time? His heart beat faster every time he thought about it. Which was every other minute.

Mrs. McKinnon was saying something to him, and he hadn't heard a word, his thoughts were so loud concerning her daughter.

"Pardon me?" he said.

Hannah McKinnon smiled. "What would you like for breakfast?"

"I can get my own. You don't have to wait on me," he said

"Don't be silly. Staying busy helps keep my mind off other things." Her smile faded, and she turned to the refrigerator. "I have bacon cooked. It will only take me a few minutes to fry or scramble eggs."

"What is your daughter having?" he asked.

Molly shot a frown in his direction. "Coffee and toast," she answered. "What's it to you?"

He nodded. "I'll have the same."

"Are you sure?" Molly's mother asked. "I really don't mind."

"Thank you, but no. I don't want to take the time," Parker said. "I'm sure we have a lot to do out at the barn."

"Don't base your breakfast on Molly's bad habits," Mrs. McKinnon said. "I'd make breakfast for her, too, if she'd let me." The older woman sighed and popped bread into the toaster. "The coffee is ready, if you'd like to help yourself. Molly can show you where the cups are. We're glad to have you in the house. I know I'll feel a lot better with you looking after our Molly."

Molly blew a sharp stream of air through her nose.

Parker chuckled. "You're the only one who'll feel better. You daughter doesn't like the idea."

Her mother spun to face Molly. "Really? I would think after yesterday's attack, you'd want someone to have your back."

Molly shot a glare at Parker. "I do. I'm just not

used to it. I've operated independently on this ranch since I can remember. It'll take some adjustment."

"Oh, sweetheart," her mother's brow wrinkled, "Parker is the nicest man. You'll have no trouble adjusting."

Parker almost laughed at the consternation written all over Molly's face. "You heard your mother. I'm the nicest man." His lips twitched, and he couldn't hold back the grin.

Molly snorted and started to say something. When her gaze rested on her mother, she must have thought better of it. "You're right, Mom. It'll be good to have someone to watch my back. And that goes for you, too. You can't even step outside this house without one of us."

"I know. I'll do my best to remain inside." She glanced out the window. "Even though it's such a beautiful day... Your father loves days like today." Her eyes grew glassy.

Parker's heart clenched. The woman had more or less lost her husband. At the very least, he was missing, and they knew he'd been tortured. If keeping busy was what helped her get through the trauma, he could help with that.

"Mrs. McKinnon, I've changed my mind. I'd love some scrambled eggs. And since Molly can't go anywhere until I'm ready, she can have some, too."

Molly stopped pouring coffee into her mug long

enough to frown at Parker. "I want to get back to that fence that needs mending."

"And we will," Parker said. "After a hearty breakfast."

"I don't—" Molly started.

As if she hadn't heard Molly, Mrs. McKinnon swiped at her eyes. "Oh, good. I'll get right on those eggs. I'm so glad you decided to eat something decent. You're getting too thin, dear."

Molly clamped her mouth shut and forced a smile. "I'm not too thin, Mom. You have to stop worrying about me."

Her mother shook her head. "I'll never stop worrying about my children. Not until I'm dead and in my grave. Even then, I hope I can keep an eye on you, if I make it to Heaven."

"You'll make it there, Mom," Molly slipped an arm around her shoulder. "You're the kindest person I know."

Molly might be irritating to Parker, but she loved her family fiercely. And her mother was right. Since her father's disappearance, Molly had lost weight. She worked hard, probably for the same reason her mother did. Staying busy kept her mind off what her father was going through.

Parker admired the McKinnons of Iron Horse. When shit happened, they came together as a unit and fought back. That was one of the reasons he liked working for James McKinnon.

They were a family, something Parker hadn't known growing up. He'd been raised by his mother, after his father deserted them. Working on a ranch had been his way of helping her with the finances. He'd sent her money when he was on active duty until the day she died of a severe case of pneumonia. She'd loved him as fiercely as Mrs. McKinnon loved her children. He missed her.

While Mrs. McKinnon scrambled eggs, Parker helped by buttering the toast and laying out forks and knives on the large kitchen table.

Molly poured another cup of coffee and handed it to him.

Their fingers touched briefly, sending a spark of awareness up his arm and into his chest.

Her eyes widened, and she jerked away her hand as if it had been burned. Had she felt it, too?

As they settled in at the table, each with a plate full of fluffy yellow scrambled eggs, Molly said, "I don't think Duncan, Fiona or Caity will be joining us."

Her mother sighed. "Caity was fussy all night long. I hope she's not coming down with something."

"Me, too. She's such a sweetie," Molly smiled. "I love my little niece. I'm so glad Fiona and Duncan are together, now."

"Me, too," Mrs. McKinnon said. "My first grandchild to spoil. Your father will be ecstatic when he learns about his first grandchild."

Molly's jaw firmed. "And he will get to see her and hold her."

Her mother nodded. "Yes, he will. I just know it."

Parker admired Mrs. McKinnon. She reminded him of his own mother. Strong, self-reliant and optimistic.

For the first few weeks her husband had been missing, the woman had been a tower of strength, convinced her husband would be coming home soon. Her confidence seemed a little more shaken after learning her husband had been tortured.

He couldn't imagine the stress she was under. Hell, he couldn't imagine the stress her husband was under.

The McKinnons were working with Hank Patterson and the Brotherhood Protectors, researching the origins of the money paid to the men who'd tortured Mr. McKinnon. When they finally sifted through the many layers of corporations, they should come up with the individual responsible for James McKinnon's disappearance.

Parker hoped they'd find the man soon. His family was holding out hope. He didn't want to see them lose that hope. And he didn't want them to lose Mr. McKinnon. The elder McKinnon had been the glue that held the Iron Horse Ranch together. Since his disappearance, his sons and daughter had stepped up to the plate to see that the ranch continued to run smoothly.

Not so worried about losing his job, Parker was more concerned for the welfare of Mr. McKinnon. He liked the man's structure and work ethic. He suspected James had had the basis of his strength and discipline even before he'd entered the Marines as a young man. The Marine Corps had cultivated even more discipline and self-control, making him the man he was today.

As a PJ, Parker had had to prove his strength and skills. He recognized and admired those qualities in others—which included all the McKinnon family.

Duncan McKinnon appeared in the doorway to the kitchen, his hair rumpled and with shadows beneath his eyes. He scrubbed a hand through his hair. "Wow. I didn't know babies could stay up all night long." He headed straight for the coffeemaker and poured some of the rich brew into a mug. Then he headed for the door. "This is for Fiona. I don't know how she managed all alone when Caity was a newborn."

"I take it the three of you won't be able to follow me into town to drop off my truck for maintenance?" Mrs. McKinnon asked.

Duncan frowned. "Is that today?"

"I can call and reschedule. Your father had it on the calendar today. It's no big deal. The factory recall can wait. It's just the side airbags, and I've turned off the functionality."

Still frowning, Duncan looked at the coffee in his

hand and back to his mother. "If it could wait, that would be better for us."

"I'll call in a few minutes," Mrs. McKinnon said.

"No. You can keep your appointment, Mom," Molly said. "I can follow you into town."

"*We* can follow you into town," Parker amended. "Better yet, Molly can drive, and I'll follow you both into town. That way I can keep an eye on you both."

"You sure?" Duncan asked. "I'd hate to take out Fiona and Caity when the little one's not feeling her best."

"You keep Caity and Fiona here at home," Mrs. McKinnon said. "Go, give that poor mama her coffee. We'll handle things."

"Keep an eye open for trouble," Parker reminded the second oldest McKinnon brother.

"I will. And thanks." Duncan left the room.

"What time is your appointment?" Molly asked. "Do we have time to take care of the animals first?"

Her mother smiled. "Plenty. It's not for a couple more hours."

Molly's lips pinched. "Will you be all right while we take care of the animals, with Duncan upstairs?"

"We're just going to the barn," Parker said. He turned to Molly. "After we drop the truck, we can head out to take care of the rest of the fence that needs repair."

Molly nodded. "We'll be within yelling distance.

And when we go out this afternoon, Duncan can stay downstairs to look out for you and his little family."

"Sounds like a plan." Mrs. McKinnon took one more bite of her scrambled eggs and rose from the table, carrying her plate to the sink.

"Mom, you didn't clean your plate," Molly said softly.

Her mother chuckled. "Oh, so now we're switching roles?"

"You haven't been eating enough to keep a bird alive," Molly said.

"I eat enough," her mother said. "Now, you two quit worrying about me. Those animals need to be tended. As for that matter, I can help."

"That won't be necessary," Parker assured her. "We can handle it."

"Unless you want to get outside," Molly suggested.

Her mother shook her head. "I'd really like to go check on my granddaughter. I worry about her."

"Then check on her," Molly said. "I can clean up the dishes."

"But you need to take care of the animals," Mrs. McKinnon argued.

"They can wait a few more minutes," Molly smiled. "I'm pretty fast at washing dishes."

"And I've pulled my share of kitchen patrol," Parker said with a smile. "I'm pretty good at drying."

Molly frowned, and then forced a smile. "We've

got this. Go check on Caity." Molly poured another mug of coffee. "And take this to Duncan. He looked like he could use it."

"He did, didn't he?" Her mother smiled. "Thank you, dear." She cupped her daughter's cheek. Then she turned to Parker. "Both of you. Thanks."

Parker dipped his head. "My pleasure, ma'am."

Mrs. McKinnon cocked an eyebrow. "Please, don't call me ma'am. It makes me feel old."

"Yes, ma'am—" Parker grinned. "Yes, Mrs. McKinnon."

"And don't call me Mrs. McKinnon. That was my mother-in-law." Her face softened. "You can call me Hannah."

Parker shook his head. "I'm sorry. I respect you too much to call you Hannah. How about Mrs. M or Mrs. Mac?"

She smiled. "That would be better," she said. "Thank you."

"No," Parker said. "Thank you. You and Mr. McKinnon have been amazing by welcoming me to this ranch and letting me do the work I do here."

"We're lucky to have you, Parker," she said. "James speaks highly of everything you do."

Parker dipped his head. "I try to do right by him. I have nothing but admiration for the man and this ranch."

"You and Molly make a good team. I've been after James for a while now to take a back seat to others when it comes to working the ranch. He's worked hard for so long that he doesn't know how to relax." Mrs. McKinnon chuckled. "I'll bet right now, he's not thinking about how miserable he is so much as what's not getting done."

"We're taking care of things," Molly said.

Her mother nodded. "He's so proud of you, Molly."

"He had a funny way of showing it," she said, tipping her head toward Parker.

Her mother gave her a soft smile. "I told him you wouldn't be happy when he hired Parker. But your father had a reason for doing what he did. He didn't want you to be saddled with all the responsibility of the ranch. Especially with all his sons serving in the military."

"It doesn't matter." Molly's lips thinned. She turned to Parker. "These dishes aren't getting done on their own."

Her mother gripped her arm. "Molly, your father wanted you to have a choice of what your life would be. If you became too entrenched in the ranch, you might not consider marriage and children. You were always so intense about doing everything here at the Iron Horse Ranch. He was afraid you wouldn't give yourself a chance to fall in love."

"I'm as good a rancher as any one of the boys," Molly said, her mouth tight.

"Better," her mother said.

Molly stared at her mother. "Dad didn't feel that way."

"He did," her mother insisted.

Molly's chin lifted, her eyes suspiciously shiny. "Can we talk about this another time?"

Parker shifted uncomfortably. He felt like he'd been caught in a conversation the two women should have had without him present. "I'll wait outside."

"If you want," Molly said. "I'm going to do the dishes." She turned back to her mother. "I've always done what I love doing. No man will ever change my mind about that. I just wish Dad would have understood that." She headed for the sink. "Are you going to dry, Parker?"

Parker gave Mrs. McKinnon a twisted grin. "We'll lock the doors behind us on our way out, just to be safe. We won't be far."

Mrs. McKinnon touched his arm and whispered, "Now, you can understand why she might not have been too happy about your coming to work at the Iron Horse Ranch. And now, she knows why her father did what he did. I'm just sorry he didn't explain it to her at the time." She dropped her hand to her side. "I hope I didn't make things even more awkward between the two of you."

"I can hear you, Mom," Molly said.

"Nothing I wouldn't say to your face," Mrs. M said. "Going to check on my grandbaby." And she left the kitchen.

Parker cringed. He didn't like being the person who had taken the job someone else deserved, no matter how well-intentioned Mr. McKinnon had been.

CHAPTER 4

MOLLY COULDN'T BELIEVE her mother had outed her in front of Parker. For the past five years, she'd gone about ranch work, trying not to show her anger over her father's choice to hire a foreman. She'd figured that, eventually, the foreman would leave, and she'd get the job.

"Look, I'm sorry your father chose me over you to be the foreman," Parker said as he lifted a hand towel from the countertop.

"I'm over it," Molly said. "I can wash and dry. You don't have to stick around. It's women's work, anyway."

"I do my own dishes in my quarters," he pointed out. "I don't consider it women's work."

"Men only do it when they have no one else to dump the task on."

"That's a very sexist thing to say," he said, taking a

wet plate from her hands. "If I'd said that, you'd have been all over me."

Molly sighed. "You're right. That was uncalled for. My brothers have done almost as many dishes as I have. My mother made sure of it. And my mother has cleaned as many stalls as any of the men who've worked on this ranch. She can pound a T-post with the best of them, and she's a better horseback rider than all of us." Molly handed him another plate. "I just wish my father would've talked to me before..."

"Before he hired me." Parker wiped the plate dry and stacked it in the cabinet.

"Yes." Molly washed another plate and handed it to him.

"You missed a spot," he said.

"Now, you're a critic?" She grabbed the plate from him and dunked it back into the sink.

He chuckled. "When I met you, I thought you were a young, cranky tomboy who wanted her daddy's attention."

Molly glared at him.

Parker held up his hands. "Don't blame me. You were angry, and I didn't know why. Now, I get it. But even before your mother set me straight, I knew you were more concerned about how well the ranch was run. You didn't counter anything I did that made sense."

"But I did tell you when you were doing something wrong," she admitted.

"Yes, you did." He reached around her, dropping a cup into the sink.

Soapy water splashed up on her, and she backed up quickly, bumping into his chest.

Heat spread up her neck into her cheeks.

"Sorry," Parker said. He turned her to face him and dabbed at the suds on the front of her shirt.

Molly's breath caught in her throat. The heat in her cheeks spread downward, filling her chest and sinking lower to her very core.

She clutched his hand with the towel. "It's just water," she said, her voice gravelly, so unlike her usual clear tone.

He raised the hand holding the towel.

Molly's eyes rounded. Was he going to kiss her fingers?

"I need the towel to dry the dishes," he said.

She let go of the breath she hadn't known she was holding. "Oh. Of course." Molly let go of his hand and the towel and spun back to the sink. She had the rest of the dishes washed quickly, her hands shaking, her mind whirling with Parker standing so near. Twice, she nearly dropped glasses while handing them off to Parker. He'd caught them both times.

"Are you okay?" he asked as she drained the soapy water from the sink.

"Yes. Why wouldn't I be?"

"You seem a little jumpy." He hung the towel on

the oven handle. "Did last night leave you a little punchy?"

"Yes," she said, a little too quickly, glad for any excuse other than Parker being near as the reason why she was so off balance. "Ready to take care of the animals?" She spun to find Parker standing right behind her.

He rested his hands on her arms. "Are you all right? I can take care of the animals myself. You can stay in the house with your mother and Duncan, if you're anxious about going outside again."

"No. I'm fine. Working with the animals always calms me. They don't usually argue or talk back." Her lips quirked. "Except when Rusty gives me attitude about his grain. He thinks I don't give him enough and tells me about it when I feed the other horses."

Parker let go of her arms and smiled. "I noticed that about him. He's got a healthy appetite."

Molly stepped around Parker. "He'd get fat if I fed him as much grain as he wanted."

"That's why he looks so good."

"Were you the one who put him up last night?" Molly's brows furrowed.

"No, your brother Bastian did."

"It's all a blur," she said.

"I don't doubt that," Parker frowned. "Whatever they gave you knocked you out."

"How did I get into the house and up to my room?" she asked. "I don't remember any of that."

"You had a little help." He held the door for her.

Molly stopped halfway through. "You carried me?"

He shrugged. "Someone had to. You weren't getting there on your own. Besides, I feel a little responsible for you now that I've saved your life." He winked and twisted the lock on the door handle.

"You know you're not responsible for me," she said.

"Uh, yes, I am." He raised his eyebrows. "Your brothers seem to think you'll listen to me over them."

Molly frowned. "They think I don't listen to them?" She snorted. "If they had something useful to say, I would. But bossing me around isn't useful."

His lips twitched. "Like they said, you don't listen to them."

"You're impossible."

"So you say." He followed her down the porch steps and out to the barn.

The horses inside their stalls whinnied impatiently.

"Sorry, boys," she called out. "I slept in."

Molly and Parker quickly went to work feeding the horses. Once they'd finished giving the horses their grain and hay, they turned them loose in the pasture beside the barn and mucked the stalls. It was dirty work, but needed to be done, since she hadn't cleaned them the day before.

When they finished mucking out the stalls, Molly

and Parker shoveled in wood chips and put fresh sections of hay in their mangers for later that day when the horses would come in from the pasture.

Once they were finished taking care of the barn, Molly grabbed a bucket of chicken feed and a fishnet and headed for the chicken coop.

"What's the net for?" Parker asked.

"For Red."

Parker's brow wrinkled. "The rooster?"

She nodded. "Yup." As she reached the chicken coop, Red the rooster charged her.

With one quick swoop, she caught the rooster in the fishnet and hung the net, rooster and all, on the side of the coop.

Parker laughed. "He doesn't usually attack me."

"For some reason, he doesn't like women," Molly said. "I learned that trick from my mother. We've had several roosters who liked to sink their spurs into our legs. This method saves our legs and the rooster from the cookpot."

Parker entered the coop with Molly.

While she poured grain into the chicken feeder, Parker collected eggs from the nests.

Between the two of them, they collected a dozen eggs, placing them in the now empty grain bucket.

Parker filled the small water trough for the chickens.

Molly left the coop with the eggs.

When they were done with the chickens, Parker

emptied the fishnet, releasing the rooster into his harem of chickens.

The rooster ruffled his feathers and strutted several steps, keeping a close eye on the man who'd turned him loose.

"Genius," Parker murmured, carrying the fishnet back to the barn where he hung it on the wall inside the door.

"Not so much genius as experience," she said. "Ever have a rooster sink his spurs into you?"

Parker shook his head. "Never got close enough."

"He waits until you're busy collecting eggs and attacks you from behind. I have scars on my calves."

"How rude," Parker said, laughter in his voice.

Molly liked it when he smiled. A little too much. "We should get back to the house and clean up before we go to town with Mom."

"Agreed." He took the bucket of eggs from her.

"I can carry that myself," she protested.

"I know you can. There's a difference between recognizing what a woman is capable of and treating her like a lady, anyway. I figure you can ride and rope better than I ever dreamed of, but you're still a woman, and my mother taught me how to treat a lady."

Molly's brow dipped further. "Why now?"

"You're the boss's daughter," he said.

"Don't give me that shit. I've always been the boss's daughter."

His jaw firmed. "You've never been attacked like you were last night. I don't ever want that to happen to you again. Not on my watch."

Her heart beat faster. "Because I'm the boss's daughter?"

He stopped, placed the bucket of eggs on the porch and pulled her into his arms. "Not because you're the boss's daughter." He tipped up her chin with one hand. "Because I made the mistake of kissing you."

Her eyes widened, and her pulse beat so fast and hard it thundered in her ears. "Mistake?"

"Yes, damn it. Mistake. Like the one I'm about to make again." Then he bent to claim her lips in a hard kiss that took her breath away. When she opened her mouth to him, he dove in, taking everything he could in that one kiss.

Molly's hands started on his chest and moved upward to wrap around his neck and bring him even closer.

They both smelled of horses and manure, and she probably had straw in her hair, but he was kissing her like there was no tomorrow.

And she was letting him.

No.

She was kissing him back like her life depended on it.

The back door opened and a startled, "Oh!" sounded before the door slammed shut again.

59

Molly backed away, her fingers covering her throbbing lips. "That was probably my mother."

"Probably."

"What am I going to say to her?" Molly asked.

"Nothing."

Molly nodded. "Right. What just happened meant nothing."

Parker frowned. "I didn't say that."

"You didn't have to." She backed away, giving him a weak, forced smile. "Come on. My mother should be ready to go to town."

He caught her arm. "Molly—"

"It's okay. You're not going to break my heart or anything. It was just a kiss." She shook free of his grip and entered the house.

Her mother stood in the kitchen filling the napkin holder in the middle of the table. "Oh, there you are. Are you two ready to follow me to town?"

"Yes, Mom. We're ready." She wanted to say more, but the lump in her throat was only getting thicker by the minute. If she didn't move soon, she might do something stupid, like cry. McKinnons did not cry. Male or female.

"Are you okay?" her mother asked, her brows forming a worried V over her nose.

"I'm fine. We should go." Molly turned her back to her mother. The woman had a sixth sense about her children. She always knew when they were unhappy or hurt.

Her mother touched her shoulder. "If you need someone to talk to later, I'm here for you."

Without turning, she covered her mother's hand. "Thanks, Mom. But I'm really okay."

"Uh huh." Her mother's fingers squeezed gently, and then released. "Am I driving?"

"No. I'll drive you in your truck. Parker will follow us to town."

"Good." Her mother looped her purse over her arm, snagged her keys from a hook on the wall and headed for the door. "That will give us time to talk."

Molly swallowed a groan. The last thing she wanted was for her mother to grill her about the kiss she'd witnessed that meant nothing.

CHAPTER 5

PARKER HADN'T LIKED the way that kiss had ended. After five years of ignoring Molly McKinnon, she had no reason to believe the kiss was anything more than what he'd claimed it was...a mistake.

When in actuality, it was so much more. The kiss seemed to be the culmination of the past five years of longing and denial.

He was supposed to protect her, not maul her. What would her father say to his foreman taking advantage of his absence to make a move on his daughter?

Nothing had seemed to matter at that moment when his lips had touched hers. He'd been where he'd longed to be from the first day he'd seen her riding in from the range, her hair having fallen out of the perpetual ponytail he'd come to know as her norm.

She'd swung out of the saddle, removed her hat

and stared him straight in the eye. "You're the new foreman?"

When he'd held out his hand, she'd ignored it, leading Rusty into the barn. "Stay out of my way. I have real work to do."

She'd walked past him, her smooth gait like that of a prized dressage horse. Her shoulders had been squared, and her slim body had been encased in faded blue jeans and a worn, red flannel shirt that had done nothing to disguise her luscious curves. Everything about that first meeting seared a permanent image in his brain.

He'd known from that day she would be trouble for him. For five years, he'd fought his desire and his attraction, knowing she wanted nothing to do with him and he'd be fired if her father knew the extent of the foreman's attraction to his daughter.

Now that he'd crossed the line, there was no going back. He wanted Molly more than he wanted to keep his job. Obviously. Otherwise, he wouldn't have kissed her. Not once, but three times, each time reminding him why he wanted to do it again.

Molly drove the truck in front of him, her mother in the passenger seat. The drive into Eagle Rock wouldn't take any more than twenty minutes on the curving roads through the Crazy Mountains.

At the first major curve going into town, Parker lost sight of the truck. For a moment his heart stood still, and he held his breath. As he rounded the curve and the truck came back in sight, he let go of the breath he'd been holding. Who would be stupid enough to launch an attack in broad daylight?

Like indoctrination training for a pararescue PJ, he forced himself to relax behind the wheel and focus on the mission. Keep the ladies safe on their way to town.

Once he could breathe easier, he thought about the kiss Mrs. M had witnessed. Molly's mother was bound to have a hundred questions for her daughter.

Parker wondered how Molly would respond. Would she say she'd enjoyed the kiss? Or would she ask her mother to butt out of her business? Or would she be noncommittal and pretend the kiss meant nothing?

His chest tightened.

The kiss might have meant nothing to her, but it had meant more than Parker was willing to admit to himself.

James McKinnon probably had bigger plans for the man he wanted to marry his only daughter. A gimpy, former Air Force PJ probably didn't rank high enough for the taciturn Marine and big ranch owner. Marines had little respect for the Air Force. They chewed them up and spit them out.

Never mind that the physical and mental requirements of making the pararescue team were challenging, and eighty percent of those who started the course washed out. He'd made the team, learning that the mental side of a mission was every bit as important as the physical side. Even more important. PJs were part of the elite Special Operations forces. Not everyone could be a PJ.

But to a battle seasoned Marine…being a PJ might not be enough to impress Mr. McKinnon when it came to his daughter.

Hell, what was he worried about? And why was he thinking he had to impress Mr. McKinnon? Molly was a McKinnon; he was the hired help. End of story.

Ahead, Molly's truck rounded another blind curve, moving out of Parker's sight.

Focus on the mission, he told himself and increased his speed to get around the corner faster so that he could once again see the truck with the two women most vulnerable to attack by the men holding the senior Mr. McKinnon.

He whipped around the curve only to find another curve snaking back in the other direction.

Again, he increased his speed, skidding sideways around the next corner. Ahead, a little further than he liked, was the truck with the two women.

Parker had just breathed a sigh when a large, dark SUV pulled out of a side road, dense with trees and overgrowth of brush.

The SUV slammed into the passenger side of the pickup and pushed it toward the edge of the road and a steep drop off.

"No!" Parker yelled and slammed his foot to the accelerator, racing toward the SUV.

Parker braced himself and rammed his truck into the left rear panel of the SUV, causing the vehicle to spin in a three-hundred-and-sixty-degree circle.

Without the SUV pushing it, the truck slowed to a stop, the front two wheels hanging over the side of the road, dangling over the drop off.

The SUV came to a stop, facing Parker's truck. Then the back wheels spun as the driver hit the accelerator hard. When the wheels gained traction, the SUV shot forward, heading straight for Parker.

Parker shifted into reverse and backed away as fast as he could, drawing the attacking SUV away from the women in the truck, hoping to give them time to right their vehicle and get back on the road.

Twisted around so that he could see behind him, Parker maneuvered his truck back around the curves in the road, at a distinct disadvantage. The SUV could move faster because it was going forward. Before too long, it would catch up to Parker and slam into him.

As he rounded the curve, Parker spun the steering wheel, sending the truck into a one-hundred-and-eighty-degree turn, leaving him facing the opposite direction.

When the SUV whipped around the curve, Parker was ready. He stood his ground, forcing the SUV to either have a head-on collision or dodge his vehicle to keep from slamming into him.

Bracing for impact, Parker waited.

At the last second, the driver of the SUV swerved around Parker's truck and sped away.

Though he would have liked to chase down the driver, Parker had to check on the women in the damaged truck. He raced forward, coming around the curve and praying he'd find the truck where he'd left it.

The road was empty. The truck was gone.

Parker skidded to a stop, leaped out of his truck and ran to the edge of the road where he'd last seen Molly and Mrs. McKinnon's vehicle.

The edge of the road dropped down a steep incline to a stand of trees fifty yards below.

That's where the truck had landed, smashed against the trunk of a tree.

At that moment, Molly crawled out the driver's window and dropped to the ground on all fours.

Parker had his cellphone out praying for reception among the hills and rock formations. Nothing.

"Mom's hurt," Molly called out from down below.

Parker scrambled down the hill, slipping and sliding in loose gravel until he reached the wreckage.

"You have to get help," Molly said, with blood on her cheek. She stared into the truck where her mother was held in place by her seatbelt. The airbag had deployed in front of her, but she had a gash on her forehead, and she remained limp.

Parker's medical training kicked in. He hurried to the other side of the vehicle and pressed his fingers to the base of her throat where he found a pulse beating.

"Is she..." Molly gulped.

"Alive? Yes."

"We have to get her out!"

"It's better to leave her where she is as long as there isn't a chance of fire. We don't know what internal or spinal injuries she might have suffered."

"You have to go for help."

Parker frowned, torn between helping Mrs. M and staying with Molly. "I don't want to leave you two."

"You have to," Molly said. "We can't stay here."

Parker knew that. He held out the gun he'd brought with him. "You know how to use this?"

She nodded. "My father made sure I knew how to handle a gun."

"Then hang on to it and shoot anyone who even thinks about threatening you." He stared into her eyes. "Do you understand?" Parker was afraid Molly was in more of a state of shock than she was letting on. But he had no choice. He had to get back up to the road and either flag someone down or continue to Eagle Rock and get the sheriff and the fire rescue team out there to retrieve Mrs. M. from where the truck had come to rest.

He scrambled up the side of the embankment, slipping and sliding all the way up. By the time he reached the top, he was breathing hard. With no other vehicles in sight, he ran to his truck, slipped in and checked his cellphone. Still no reception.

Without wasting another minute, he shifted into drive and jammed his foot to the accelerator, sending him flying toward town. All along the way, he kept checking his cellphone, praying for reception.

A mile out of Eagle Rock, he finally got a signal. Slowing to a stop on the side of the road, he pressed 911.

Dispatch answered. After Parker gave her the details and location, the woman said she'd send assistance and a mountain rescue team. Within minutes, Parker could hear the wail of sirens as the fire department and ambulance left their stations and headed toward him.

Parker made a U-turn in the middle of the highway and raced back to the position where he'd left Molly and Mrs. M.

He parked his truck on the side of the road and engaged his hazard lights. Then he scrambled back down the hillside, praying nothing had happened to Molly and her mother while he'd been away.

As he slid to a halt beside the crashed truck, Molly came out of the shadows of the tree, holding the gun he'd given her. "Oh, thank God," she cried and threw her arms around his neck.

"How's she doing?" he asked.

"Same as when you left," Molly said. "She's still unconscious. I'm afraid, Parker. What if she has internal injuries? What if she has bleeding on the brain?" Molly shook her head. "My father's missing… I can't lose my mother, too."

The sirens indicated the arrival of the firetruck and the ambulance.

Men scrambled down the steep hill, carrying a rescue litter and what looked like a toolbox filled with medical supplies.

After trying the doors on both sides of the truck, one of the rescue team radioed back to the men up on the road that they would need the jaws of life to extract the crash victim.

Parker stood out of the way, holding Molly in his arms, letting the rescue workers do their job.

Molly wrapped an arm around his waist and leaned against him, her body trembling.

"You need to let the medics check you out as well," Parker said.

"I'm fine," she insisted.

"You're shaking like a leaf."

"Can I help it that it's cold out here?" she said through chattering teeth.

"Sweetheart, it's not that cold. I'm betting that shock is setting in." His arm tightened around her.

"Come on. Let's get you up to my truck. I have a blanket in the back seat."

She shook her head. "I can't leave my mother."

"They're bringing her out. We need to get out of the way and not create more work for them to manage."

Molly nodded. "Okay," she said. "But I'm riding to the hospital with her."

"I'm sure they'll let you. And I'll follow you two."

While they waited what felt like a very long time for them to bring Mrs. M up the side of the hill, Parker held Molly wrapped in the blanket he kept in his truck.

Soon, she stopped shaking.

By the time Mrs. M was brought to the top, Molly was more in control of herself and able to climb into the back of the ambulance on her own.

Parker followed the ambulance all the way to Bozeman, where Mrs. M was delivered to the emergency room.

In the ER waiting room, Parker made the call to Hank Patterson.

"Brotherhood Protectors, Hank Patterson speaking."

"Hank, Parker Bailey, foreman at the Iron Horse Ranch. I'm not sure if the McKinnons have engaged your team yet, but we need help."

"Angus called me a little while ago, saying he

could use some help keeping an eye on the ranch. I have a couple of guys I can assign today."

"We'll need someone at the hospital in Bozeman to guard Mrs. McKinnon."

"Give me the sitrep," Hank said, his voice tight.

Parker detailed the attack on the road into Eagle Rock. "I don't think she's safe lying in a hospital without some protection."

"I'm sending Boomer, a Navy SEAL. He'll be there as soon as I can get him on the road."

Parker ended the call and hit the number for Angus McKinnon.

"Parker, what's going on?" Angus asked. "I just got to the ranch, and my mother and Molly aren't here. I take it they're with you?"

Parker went through the incident again with Angus. "Patterson is sending someone to guard your mother at the hospital. I don't yet know the extent of her injuries, but they're bound to keep her for observation, if nothing else. She was unconscious when they brought her in. Molly is a bit banged up, but she says she's okay."

Angus swore. "Bree and I will be there as soon as we can. I'll notify the others."

"We'll be here." Parker looked up as Molly came out of the restricted area, her face drawn and with the cut on her forehead covered with a butterfly bandage. Her hair had worked loose of her ponytail, and her eyes were red-rimmed, but she was still the most beautiful woman Parker had ever seen. Inside and out.

Parker opened his arms, and she walked into them, laying her cheek on his chest.

"HOW MUCH MORE CAN MY family take?" Molly whispered, glad to be held in Parker's arms.

"I don't know," Parker answered, stroking her hair and holding her. "I'm at a loss for what to do. You McKinnons have been through a lot over the past few weeks. It seems every member of the family has had some crisis to overcome, with the biggest being your missing father, the cornerstone of the Iron Horse Ranch."

"Tell me about it," Molly said.

"How's your mother?" Parker asked.

"They're taking her back for x-rays, a CT scan and MRI. She woke briefly and asked where she was." Molly shook her head, her fingers curling into Parker's shirt. "She was more worried about being home for when Dad returns than finding out the extent of her own injuries."

"What about you?" Parker tipped up her chin. "Did they check you over?"

She nodded. "I'm fine. A bruise across my chest where the seatbelt tightened and bump on the head, but no concussion. The airbag saved me. We should've fixed the side airbags sooner on that truck.

The front airbags deployed and saved us from a lot more trauma. Mom's injuries are from when the SUV T-boned us on the highway. Her side of the vehicle took the brunt of the impact. I suspect at the very least she has some broken ribs and who knows what else." Molly wrapped her arms around Parker's waist. She didn't care if he was just being nice. She needed human contact. No. She needed contact with him. "I just want this all to end, and for Mom and Dad to come home healthy."

"We all want that," Parker said.

In the next thirty minutes, the waiting room filled with McKinnons.

Angus and his fiancée, Bree, arrived first.

"Duncan is staying at the house with Fiona and baby Caity," Angus said. "Otherwise he'd be here."

Molly gave her brother a weak smile. "I'm sure Mom would prefer they kept the baby at home."

Colin and Emily burst through the door next, followed by Bastian and Jenna.

"How's Mom?" Angus asked.

"We're waiting to hear," Parker said, his arm remaining around Molly's waist.

Molly was pleased he hadn't moved away. The closer he was, the better she felt. Especially after watching her life pass before her eyes as that SUV had pushed their truck off the road. She'd never felt so helpless.

"How are you, Molls?" Angus asked.

Molly leaned into Parker. "I'm fine. But I've had enough of this. We have to find Dad and put an end to this attack on our entire family."

Angus's lips thinned into a tight line. "We're trying. Hank's computer guy, Swede, is working night and day, trying to figure out the people behind the payment made to Otis Ferguson. Whoever paid him to torture Dad has got to be the one holding him hostage. From what Hank says, we're close."

Molly shook her head. "Not close enough. Who are we going to lose next? Mom? Me? Baby Caity?" She pointed to Angus. "You? I'm sick of this. If I have to search every square inch of the county myself, I'm going to find the son of a bitch and make him pay for all the heartache and pain he's caused our family."

Hank Patterson entered the waiting room with a broad-shouldered man with black hair and gray eyes. He stopped in front of Angus. "This is Brandon Rayne. He'll stand guard over your mother while she's in the hospital."

Rayne held out his hand to the oldest brother. "Call me Boomer." He shook Angus's hand, and then Parker's, Molly's, Colin's and Bastian's. Finally, he looked around. "Have they assigned her a room, yet?"

Molly shook her head. "No. They took her to have x-rays, a CT scan and an MRI."

"I'd like to be back there with her. Given the circumstances, I want her within my sight at all times."

Angus walked Boomer to the reception desk. Moments later, Boomer was escorted past the restricted door, and Angus returned to the others. "They only allow one person at a time back there. The nurse said the doctor will be out shortly."

"We've had some movement on the hacking into the corporation based out of Bozeman," Hank announced. "The corporation is in name only. There's no physical location or buildings associated with it, just a bank account. My computer guy, Swede, is tiptoeing through the bank's databases, searching for the connections."

"Is tiptoeing code for hacking?" Parker asked.

Hank held up his hands. "We're doing what we can. Swede has some connections on the dark web also looking for the origin of the money. A bank account has to have an original source for any money transferred into it. Apparently, the money was bounced around to several foreign banks before it landed in the Caymans. One at a time, Swede is following the breadcrumbs. It just takes time."

"We're running out of time," Molly said. "What else can we do? Turn the entire county upside down, search every home and building?"

"That takes time as well, and no one has that kind of manpower," Angus said. "You know the Crazy Mountains. They're full of hiding places. Whoever has our father is likely moving him every day or so to keep anyone from finding him."

"We can't do this forever," Molly said. "And Dad won't survive much longer if they're torturing him every day."

Hank nodded. "True. We're doing the best we can. I've assigned two of my guys to watch over your family at the ranch. They should be getting there, right about now. I called Duncan and let him know to expect Taz and Kujo. Kujo comes with a retired military war dog, Six. They'll protect your family home. I'll bring in two more to change shifts, as needed."

"Thank you," Angus said. "At this point, I'm not sure who they'll target to get our father to talk. It could be any one of us."

"I think it's time we searched the hills again," Colin said.

"Jenna and I have been researching the abandoned buildings and ghost towns left by miners. We've been in a number of derelict houses and mine offices." Bastian shook his head. "Nothing, so far. We're also looking for locations where that money could've been hidden. Find the money, and they'll have no need to torture our father anymore."

"Maybe we should be looking in active buildings, homes, offices. He has to be out there," Molly said. "He's probably right under our noses, and we just can't see."

"Are we doing this wrong?" Angus asked. "Should we make it more convenient for someone to abduct one of us? Instead of holing up and keeping our heads down, shouldn't we be out and about, giving Dad's captors a shot at us?"

"Are you kidding me?" Parker broke into the family discussion. "They almost got Molly. You want them to get your mother or sister?"

Angus shook his head. "No, of course not. But one of us, armed with a GPS tracking device, could lead the rest of us to where they're keeping Dad. We can follow the tracker."

"I don't like it," Molly said. "What if Dad really doesn't know where that money is? What if they torture one of us to death, and Dad still can't tell them? What does that buy us? One dead sibling, possibly a dead father and a grieving family." She shook her head. "No."

"So, we're back to square one and relying on the computer genius to find that link that'll lead us to who has our father." Angus sighed. "It's not enough."

"I'm going back out in the hills," Colin said. "Who's with me?"

Bastian raised a hand. "As long as Hank's Brotherhood Protectors are keeping things safe at the ranch house with our ladies, I'll go with you."

At that moment, the restricted door opened, and a man in a physician's white coat came out. "McKinnon family?" he said, glancing around the waiting room.

All eight of them crowded around the doctor.

The man's eyes got big, and he smiled. "We checked Mrs. McKinnon over and didn't find anything major, besides a concussion and a broken rib. She's bruised and will experience some pain, but there's no reason we can't release her in the morning, as long as she doesn't show any signs of head trauma. Based on Miss McKinnon's report of the accident, your mother is lucky to be alive and in as good of shape as she is. Any questions?"

"No, sir," Angus said. "Thank you for taking good care of her."

The doctor left and a nurse took his place.

"Mrs. McKinnon is moving to a room on the second floor. Her bodyguard will accompany her. Once she's settled, she'll be allowed visitors. That should be in about twenty minutes." She gave them the room number and excused herself.

"I'm staying here tonight," Molly declared.

"You don't have to," Angus said. "Boomer will make sure no one gets to her."

"That's not why I want to stay. She's in a hospital. She might be scared after what happened. I know I've been scared since they made an attempt to take me yesterday. She needs one of us with her. And I think I'm the best candidate for the job." She lifted her chin. "Besides, you all have your loved ones to take care of. I don't." Her gaze swept over Parker.

"Okay. But don't go anywhere outside Mom's

room. Boomer can't watch out for both of you, if you go galivanting all over the hospital," Angus said.

"I'm staying, too," Parker announced. "Boomer and I will make sure your mother and sister remain safe."

Angus's eyes narrowed. "As long as you're sure. Bastian and Colin can take care of the animals."

Parker nodded, his gaze on Molly. "We took care of them this morning. All you need to do is move the horses to their stalls. Their hay is already there."

"Easy enough," Bastian said. "I'd feel better with more people here."

"If you need another guard on the door," Hank said, "let me know."

"We'll manage tonight," Parker said.

Molly's heart warmed, and her fear dissipated, knowing that Parker would be with her at the hospital through the night.

They couldn't take anything for granted. Not anymore. Every nurse who came through the door, every doctor, would have to provide credentials in order to gain access to Molly's mother.

Molly would make certain no one got to her mother on her watch. And having Parker close was a bonus she wouldn't turn down. Especially knowing how well he could kiss.

CHAPTER 6

ALL EIGHT OF the McKinnon group took the elevator up one floor and stopped at the nurses' station.

Parker stood back as the McKinnon siblings asked about their mother.

"Only two can go to your mother's room at a time," the nurse said.

"Jenna and I will go first," Bastian said. "Then Colin and Emily. That way we can get back to the ranch and take care of the animals for the evening."

Bastian held Jenna's hand as they walked down the hallway to his mother's room.

"The rest of you can take a seat in the waiting room lounge around the corner," the nurse said.

"Thank you," Molly said.

As soon as he entered the lounge, Parker walked to the coffee pot in the corner and stared down into a carafe where the coffee had evaporated, leaving a dark ring around the bottom of the glass. He sighed.

"Need a cup of coffee?" Molly asked.

"Desperately," he responded.

"We can go down to the cafeteria and get a fresh cup," Molly suggested.

"Whatever you want to do," he said. "I'm your shadow."

"I need coffee." She glanced around at her brothers, still in the lounge. "Anyone else need coffee?"

All three of her brothers nodded. Jenna, Bree and Emily shook their heads.

"I'll get a bottle of water from the machine in the hallway," Bree said.

"Same," Jenna agreed.

"I think I saw apple juice. But, thanks, Molly," Emily said.

"I'll bring back what I can," Molly said. "It'll be black."

"That's the only kind of coffee, isn't it?" Bastian said.

Molly nodded as they moved down the hallway.

"You like your coffee black?" Parker asked.

"My brothers taught me to drink coffee at a young age. Strong and black. No milk or sugar. When they told me it would put hair on my chest, I drank it anyway, wanting to be like my big brothers. Besides, they were always feeding me some bullshit, teasing me because I was younger than they were, gullible and always trying to please. I resented being a girl and the youngest of the clan. Until they all left for the military."

Parker took her hand and closed his fingers around hers. "Is that when you came into your own?"

She nodded. "Pretty much. That's when I realized my own value. There wasn't anyone else to do the work they'd been doing. I had been doing it, too, right alongside them, but no one seemed to notice."

"Especially your father?"

"Especially him," she said, staring at the corridor in front of her. "For the longest, I resented being female and that my father would never look at me the same way he looked at his sons. I even thought about joining the military, just to be more like them. And I would have, but after they left, my father needed the help. He started relying on me to do the work, no matter how hard."

"I'm glad you're female," Parker said. "You're every bit as good a rancher as any of your brothers, if not better."

"Better," Molly said. "I've been at it longer than any of them."

"What if they decide to leave the military and come back to the ranch?" Parker asked as they stepped into the elevator and pushed the button for the cafeteria floor.

Molly shrugged. "I've been doing this long enough I no longer feel the need to prove myself to anyone. I know what I'm capable of." She smiled. "And I look forward to being an aunt to all the nieces and nephews they'll bring to me."

"What about you? Don't you want children?"

Molly's cheeks turned pink. "I haven't really thought about having children."

"Wouldn't they keep you from being out on the range, mending fences, helping birth calves, hauling hay?" He'd seen how she did everything any ranch hand would do and more. "Would you give that up to have babies?"

She frowned. "I don't know. The question never came up. I'd have to think about it."

"You like kids. I've seen you with Caity. She loves you."

"And I adore her," Molly said with a smile. "She's amazing and learns so quickly. I can't wait to teach her how to ride a horse."

"Wouldn't you like to teach your own little girl how to ride a horse?"

For a long moment, she didn't answer, but her lips curved in a smile. "I guess." She frowned and shot a glance toward Parker as he held her hand. "What about you? You have to be in your thirties, by now. Why aren't you married with a couple of kids of your own?"

He shrugged. "Never seemed to be the right time or the right woman. On active duty, I was gone a lot to war zones. The girls I dated weren't willing to wait around until I returned. Some didn't like the idea of me going into harm's way over and over. They all ended up settling for men with regular jobs, like package delivery men, accountants and bar owners. None of those guys deployed to the other side of the world or were shot at as often.

"I don't know." Molly chuckled. "Package delivery guys are attacked often by dogs and bar owners have their share of fights and shootings. I'm not sure about accountants. They might have their own clients who go nuts when they discover how much they owe in taxes."

Parker smiled and shook his head. "You get the picture."

"You've been out of the service for five years. Why haven't you found someone to settle down with?"

"I was busy learning the job and taking care of a huge ranch with the help of the boss and his competent daughter." He squeezed her hand, liking the way it felt in his. Hers wasn't as soft as some of the women he'd dated. She had calluses from mucking stalls and a strong grip. He liked that she wasn't weak and didn't run screaming when confronted by a snake. And she wasn't afraid to get dirt under her fingernails.

He liked Molly McKinnon. A lot. Maybe too much.

The elevator door opened, and they proceeded to

the cafeteria where Molly found a tray and loaded it with cups of fresh coffee.

When they had all they needed, Parker paid for their purchases and took the tray from Molly.

"Again, I can carry the tray."

"Again, I know you're fully capable of carrying an eighty-pound bale of hay. That's not the point. The point is that my mama taught me to be a gentleman. Unless you've had a sex change, you're still a female." He leaned his head close to her ear and added, "And I, for one, am glad you are."

Molly's cheeks turned pink again.

He grinned, liking that he could make her blush so easily. She might want to be more like her brothers, but she was female through and through.

Back in the lounge, Parker laid the tray on a table and took a cup for himself. Molly claimed one, and then Angus and Colin took one each.

Bastian entered the room with Jenna and made a beeline to the last cup of coffee. "Thank God."

"How was she?" Colin asked.

Bastian took a careful sip and answered, "Banged up, but alive and kicking."

Colin laughed. "That's Mom, all over. It takes a lot to bring her down." He turned to Emily. "Ready?"

She capped her bottle of apple juice, slid it into her purse and nodded. "Ready."

They left the lounge for their time with Mrs. McKinnon.

A man walked past the lounge, heading to the nurse's station.

"Isn't that Lewis Griffith?" Angus asked.

Molly nodded. "What's he doing here?"

"Who is Lewis Griffith?" Parker asked.

"He and his wife own the Lucky Lady Lodge," Molly said.

A moment later, Griffith entered the lounge. "Sorry. I didn't see you when I passed by." Lewis walked up to Angus first and held out his hand. "I was in Bozeman when I got word about Hannah's accident. They wouldn't tell me anything at the nurse's station. Is she okay?"

Angus shook the man's hand and nodded. "She's going to be okay. Whoever did this to her won't be when we get our hands on him." Angus's mouth firmed into a tight line.

"I'm sure. I hear someone came out of a side road and hit the truck?" Griffith shook his head. "Who would have done such a thing?"

Bastian snorted. "The same person who's been terrorizing our family since my father disappeared."

"I was sorry to hear about the loss of your father," Griffith said. "Has the sheriff come up with any clues as to his whereabouts?"

"No," Molly said.

"Well, if there's anything I can do to help, please don't hesitate to contact me." He pulled a business card out of his wallet and handed it to Angus. "We're sponsoring a fundraiser dinner and dance at the lodge to help save the old building. The historical society of Montana has deemed it in need of repair to retain its historical significance. We have to come up with the money to do it or sell. I know how much your mother loves the old lodge. If she's up to it, I'd love to see her at the fundraiser."

"I'll let her know," Angus said.

"I promise no sales pressure. Just a get-together of neighbors who care about the lodge." He held out his hand to Angus again. "Please give your mother my condolences and let her know I wish her a full and speedy recovery."

Angus nodded. "I will."

Silence reigned in the lounge until the elevator button dinged down the hallway.

Colin shook his head. "'How does a man like that think it appropriate to advertise his fundraiser when our mother has been attacked and is now laid up in the hospital?"

"Mom has always been the first one to help the community in times of need," Molly said. "She loves the old lodge. She worked there as a girl, waiting tables at the restaurant for tip money."

"Still, he could have waited until she was back on her feet and home before asking her to attend a fundraiser to save his lodge," Colin grumbled.

Bastian and Jenna returned to the lounge.

"Mom's a little tired. I think they gave her something for pain, and it's making her sleepy," Bastian said.

"Bree and I will only take a minute. I want her to know we're here for her and we love her." Angus cupped Bree's arm and led her down the hall to his mother's room.

"We're going to take off to make sure the animals are taken care of," Colin said. "And I'm sure Duncan would like to know how Mom's doing." He hugged Molly. "I'm glad you're all right."

"Thanks," Molly hugged her brother back and smiled up into his eyes. "Thanks for taking care of the animals."

"Are you kidding? You do so much around the place, I barely get to help." He kissed her forehead. "Thank you for all you do and for taking care of Mom and Dad while we've been away."

Bastian hugged Molly next. "Glad you're okay, Sis." He rubbed his knuckles over her hair. "I don't know who'd I pick on if you weren't around."

Molly rolled her eyes. "Glad I can help out."

"No, really," he said with a grin. "You're my favorite sister."

She snorted. "I'm your *only* sister."

"And the best one a brother could ever have." He gave her a bear hug that lifted her off the ground, and then kissed her forehead. As he passed Parker, his eyes narrowed. "Take care of Molls. Like she said, she's the only sister we have."

Parker nodded. "I'll be here."

Colin, Emily, Bastian and Jenna left the lounge. A moment later the elevator button dinged, and they were on their way down to ground level and home.

Angus returned with Bree. "Mom's asleep. Boomer is seated in a chair outside her door. No one's getting past him. You could come back to the ranch and get some rest. I bet you're exhausted after all that's happened yesterday and today."

Molly was shaking her head before her brother finished his sentence. "I'm staying. Mom needs one of us here when she wakes. I'd like it to be me."

Angus nodded.

"Call us if you need us to come give you a break," Bree said. "We love you, Molly, and we're glad you're okay."

Molly hugged her brother's fiancée. "Thanks, Bree. I love you, too."

When Angus and Bree were gone, the lounge was quiet.

Parker pulled Molly into his arms and held her close. "Your mother's going to be okay."

Molly nodded. "I know. I hate it when I get all weepy. McKinnons don't cry."

"You're allowed."

She snorted. "Because I'm female?"

"No, because you care so much." He tipped up her chin. "Don't tell anyone, but I cried several times when I was a member of the pararescue team."

Her eyebrows drew together. "You did?"

His chest tightened as he nodded. "I cried when one of my buddies was shot. He was right next to me. The bullet missed me and hit him. I held him in my arms as he bled out."

"You couldn't save him?" Molly asked, her voice a soft whisper.

Parker shook his head. "He was hit in the heart. There was nothing I could do."

"Is that why you got out?"

He shook his head. "I was medically discharged after I took shrapnel to the knee, among other places. I cried during that mission, too."

"Because you were hit?" she asked.

"No." He stared at the far corner of the lounge. "I wasn't able to save the pilot I was sent in to recover. He had a wife and two small children waiting for him at home."

Molly cupped his cheek. "You can't be expected to save everyone."

"It was my job. What I did. And I failed."

Molly wrapped her arms around his waist and rested her cheek against his chest. "It's how I feel about my father. I've failed him because I can't find him."

"That's different."

"No, it's not. It's my responsibility to find him. I keep thinking I should have let those guys take me, then, at least, I'd know where my father was located, and I'd find a way out of there with him."

Parker shook his head. "No. Don't ever think that way. They drugged you. You never could've escaped if they'd continued to drug you. And, like your brother said, if your father really doesn't know where that money is, his captors would kill you after torturing you, and then kill your father." He kissed the tip of her nose. "Now that I know what it's like to kiss you, I don't want to stop. Don't make me stop."

He bent and claimed her mouth in meeting of the lips that started out gentle. As the kiss progressed, Molly slipped her hands around his neck and pulled him closer as she rose up on her toes. She opened to him, sliding her tongue past his teeth to caress his.

Parker held her for a long time, the kiss the only coherent thought in his head. When it ended, he continued to hold her close, knowing everything had changed. Especially him. Molly McKinnon was a woman worth fighting for. A woman who could stand at his side as an equal, yet had a soft body made for loving.

If only she wasn't the boss's daughter.

The thought crossed his mind and he immediately dismissed it. She was worth fighting for. If the boss had a problem with the foreman dating his daughter, Parker would find another job. He could go to work for the fire department as an EMT or go back to school and get his nursing degree. He'd been good as a medic with the PJs, and he had the GI bill to pay for the courses. He'd do whatever it took to prove to Molly he was good enough for her.

And he'd prove to Mr. McKinnon that he was good enough for his daughter. He respected James McKinnon, and he didn't want him to lose him as a boss and a friend, nor did he want to alienate himself to Molly's father, a man she loved.

Parker shook his head. He wouldn't know how Mr. McKinnon might feel about him dating his daughter until the man returned. Parker would rather have his blessing than lose the man's friendship altogether.

"Ready to go see my mother?" Molly asked, leaning away from him.

He nodded and followed her down the hall.

Boomer stood beside a chair, doing squats. He grinned as they stopped in front of him. "Might as well get some exercising in while I'm here."

"Bored?"

"Not at all. I was just thinking how peaceful it is. I have a baby at home." His smile broadened. "I rarely have peace. Don't get me wrong. I love Maya to the moon and back, but she has a lot of energy and demands attention all the time."

"She sounds amazing," Molly said. "You need to get her together for a playdate with Caity. The two would have a ball."

"I'll do that. Daphne wants to get to know some of the moms in the area."

"Anyone besides my brothers come by?" Molly asked.

Boomer shook his head. "Once the nurse gave your mother the sedative, she's been too groggy to keep her eyes open. I checked on her a few minutes ago; she was sound asleep."

"Thank you," Molly said and slipped into the room.

Parker followed, letting the door swing closed behind them.

Mrs. M lay against the white sheets, her face pale, eyes closed. She had an IV attached to her arm and monitors displaying the steady, reassuring beat of her heart.

Molly leaned over the bed and brushed a brief kiss to her mother's cheek. "I love you, Mom."

Her mother didn't respond.

Molly nodded toward a lounge chair. "You can have the comfy chair. I'll take the window seat cushion. I think I can stretch out on it better than you can."

Parker shook his head. "You take the lounge chair. It's closer to your mother. She'll want to see your bright shining face more than mine."

"Okay, but only for a little while." Molly settled into the lounge chair, her gaze capturing his. "When we decide to sleep, we'll switch."

"Deal." He leaned over her and adjusted the chair, lifting her legs. "While your mother is sleeping, you should close your eyes. You were in that accident as well."

"I might just do that." Molly reached up and hooked the back of his neck before he could straighten. "Thank you for taking such good care of us."

Parker brushed her lips with his. "If I'd taken such good care of you, your mother wouldn't be in the hospital right now."

Molly shook her head. "You couldn't have seen that SUV coming. He was waiting and somehow knew we would be there. You weren't even around that curve yet."

"I should have been following closer."

"No. It wasn't safe to follow that close." She touched a finger to his lips. "What's done is done. Mom's going to be okay. We'll be home tomorrow, and we can get back to searching for Dad."

Parker straightened and paced the room. He too felt the frustration. Too many weeks had already passed since Mr. McKinnon's disappearance. Something had to give. And he refused to let it be Molly or her mother's capture and subsequent torture to get McKinnon to talk.

Molly closed her eyes.

While she slept, Parker studied her. Her long auburn hair lay in waves around her shoulders, and her eyelashes made dark crescents against her tanned cheeks. The woman who'd tried to be as tough and masculine as her brothers fell way short of her goal. Every curve of her face and body were absolutely feminine and beautiful.

For over an hour, she slept, her face soft, her body relaxed. All that time, Parker watched her and her mother, envying their closeness. Seeing their love for each other, reminded him of his mother and how much she'd loved him. Molly loved her mother and father as fiercely as she attacked every challenge in her life.

"She's special," a soft, gravelly voice said. Molly's mother's gaze went from him to her daughter who slept on.

Parker's gaze shot to Mrs. M. "Yes, she is," he whispered, careful not to wake Molly.

He moved around to the other side of Mrs. M's bed and lifted her hand. "How are you feeling?"

"Other than a bit of a headache, I'm fine." She struggled, trying to sit up. "I need to get home and start supper."

Parker chuckled. "No, ma'am. You need to lay back and relax. You have a concussion. If all goes well tonight, they'll let you go home in the morning."

"What happened?" she asked, pinching the bridge of her nose.

"Someone T-boned your vehicle on the road into Eagle Rock."

Her gaze shot to her daughter. "Molly?"

"Is fine. Just a little bump on her forehead. We were more worried about you."

"I'm fine. I just need to get home. All those people in my house. I need to make supper."

"They can fend for themselves," Parker assured her.

Mrs. M lay back against the pillow and looked up at Parker. "You're right. They're adults. They can make supper. At the very least, the boys can grill some mean steaks—if they think to thaw them out first." She shook her head. "What about you and Molly? Why didn't you go home to be with them?"

"Molly insisted we stay with you tonight. She didn't want you to wake up to an empty room."

Tears welled in Mrs. M's eyes. "She's got a heart the size of the Montana skies. She's special." The older woman chuckled. "I'm repeating myself, aren't I?" She drew in a deep breath and let it out wincing. "Broken rib?"

Parker nodded. "So the doctor said."

"I remember how it feels. I broke a rib back before I was pregnant with Bastian. Was thrown from a horse. James was so upset that he wanted to get rid of the horse. I told him if he got rid of the horse, he might as well get rid of me, too. It wasn't the horse's fault he threw me. He saw a snake. It spooked him, and he did everything in his power to get away from it quickly. That horse went on to be my favorite. Had him until he was twenty-five years old. Molly learned to ride on him when she was three."

Parker reached for Mrs. M's hand. "That must be where Molly got her spirit of adventure."

Mrs. M nodded. "My husband loves us, but he likes to follow rules, and everything needs to be regimented to make him happy. I'm afraid I'm more of a free spirit. Sometimes, it frustrates him. But I think we all need someone to balance us." She looked up at Parker. "Do you balance Molly?"

"I don't know. You know her better than I do," he said, speaking softly, enjoying his conversation with Molly's mother.

"She likes to break the rules, which frustrates my husband. She's willing to try things in a different way to improve processes and bring things up to the twenty-first century. I'm so proud of all she's done for the Iron Horse Ranch."

"She's amazing and a talented horsewoman."

"And she's good with children." Her mother sighed. "She needs some of her own. She'd make a wonderful mother. She'd teach her daughters to be independent and to go wherever their dreams lead them."

"You don't have to convince me. I think she'd be good with her own kids," Parker said, his gaze on the woman sleeping in the lounge chair. He could imagine her with a swollen belly, her cheeks flushed and her eyes sparkling. She'd be beautiful pregnant.

"I hope someone will love her as she deserves to be loved."

His gaze went back to the older woman. "And how is that?"

"With all his heart. Because Molly is one of those people who goes all in on everything she does. If she loves someone, she loves with all of her heart."

MOLLY STIRRED in the chair on the other side of her mother's bed, opening her eyes. "Hey," she said, her voice froggy with sleep. "How are you feeling?"

"I'm feeling fine," her mother said. "You look tired. Maybe we should trade places?"

Molly smiled at her mother, lowered her feet to the ground and stood, stretching her arms above her head. "Trust me, the doctors have the right person in the hospital bed." She looked across at Parker. "Did I sleep long?"

He nodded. "Over an hour."

"You must have needed it," her mother said. "You had a terrible experience last night."

"I survived. Yours was worse. You were unconscious when they carried you up the hill to the ambulance. Do you remember any of that?"

Her mother shook her head. "Up a hill?"

"Yes."

Mrs. M frowned. "I don't remember anything. Was it bad?"

Molly patted her hand. "It could have been worse," her voice cracked. She swallowed hard and continued. "The good news is you'll get to go home in the morning, if you behave yourself."

"Thank goodness," Molly's mother said. "I need to check on Caity. I hope she's feeling better."

"I'll call in a minute and check in with Duncan. In the meantime, are you hungry? Want me to see what they'll let you have for dinner?"

"That would be lovely." Mrs. M winked at Molly. "I am a little hungry."

"Done." Molly headed for the door. "I'll be back in a minute."

"*We* will be back in a minute," Parker said. "Wait for me."

Molly shook her head. "We're in a hospital. I can go to the nurses' station without a bodyguard."

"What did you promise me?" Parker reminded her.

With a sigh. "That I wouldn't try to shake you." She rolled her eyes. "See what I have to put up with?" Molly smiled at her mother. "You have your own bodyguard outside your door. His name is Boomer. Be nice to him. He's got a baby girl who might come play with Caity."

Her mother's face lit up. "Please, tell him to come

in. I'd like to meet this young man. Caity needs a playmate."

Molly chuckled on her way out.

Parker smiled. Mrs. M always had others in mind, never herself. He liked her. Always had. Mr. McKinnon struck gold when he married her. She was his balance.

Could Parker be Molly's balance?

He followed her out of the room, mulling through the redhead's traits and his own. He didn't see it, but Mrs. M could...?

CHAPTER 7

"Boomer," Molly stopped in front of the man standing outside her mother's hospital room. "My mother requests the pleasure of your company." Her lips tugged at the corners. If Boomer wasn't already involved with someone, her mother would have him married off in a heartbeat. Whatever his relationship status, the McKinnon matriarch would know within the first five minutes of grilling him.

"I almost feel sorry for Boomer," she murmured as the big, former Navy SEAL entered the room and closed the door behind him.

"Why?"

"My mother is relentless when it comes to getting to know everything there is to know about someone." As she passed Parker, her shoulder brushed against his chest. Her heartbeat stuttered, and a flush of heat washed over her.

Molly could feel Parker's gaze boring into her back. She wondered if she was walking weird or like a jock. Then she shrugged and forced herself to remain calm. Parker was just a man, not a critic of all things female.

Wait. Wasn't that what all men were? Critics of all things female?

Her thoughts were taking her to places she'd rather not go. Painting all men with the same brush went against her grain. Parker wasn't all men. He was the foreman of the Iron Horse Ranch, and he'd been assigned to act as her bodyguard.

If he happened to kiss her, well then, that was a perk.

The nurse at the station smiled at Parker before she turned to Molly and let her smile slip. "How can I help you?" As soon as she asked the question, she turned back to Parker and her smile blossomed.

Molly's fists clenched. "Mrs. McKinnon is awake. Is it possible for her to get something to eat?"

"Absolutely." The nurse handed her a menu. "She can have anything on the menu." She pointed to a phone number. "Just call that number and place your order. It could take up to forty-five minutes, depending on how busy they are in the kitchen. Guests are invited to order as well. It's self-explanatory. Let me know if you have any questions. I'd be happy to help." Again, she smiled at Parker.

"Thank you." Molly took the menu and marched back to her mother's room.

"What's wrong?" Parker asked as he hurried to catch up.

"Nothing," Molly said, her voice tight, her fists still clenched.

"If nothing's wrong, why are you mad?" He took her hand and unfurled her fist.

"I don't know. It doesn't matter." His holding her hand made the butterflies in her belly flutter. She tugged on her hand, but he refused to release it.

"Are you angry because the nurse was flirting with me?"

"No," she said, her answer a little too quick. "You don't belong to me. Why should I be mad?"

A smile curved his lips, and lights danced in his eyes. "No reason." He let go of her hand and knocked on her mother's door.

"Come in," her mother's voice called out, strong and clear.

"She's obviously feeling better," Molly muttered.

Boomer pushed out of the lounge chair beside the bed. "Your mother was just entertaining me with stories about growing up in Eagle Rock. Maya will have a great childhood here, if she does half the things your mother did."

"I'll have Fiona call Daphne to set up a playdate soon with Caity and Maya," Molly's mother said. "They're getting big enough to interact with each other. They'll eventually be going to school together."

"I'll let Daphne know. And thanks." Boomer left the room.

After Molly showed her mother the menu, they placed her order.

"You two don't have to stay here with me. I can order a meal for Boomer, and he can eat with me. Why don't you two take advantage of being in the big city of Bozeman and go out to dinner."

Molly glanced down at her dirty clothes. "I'm not dressed to eat out."

"Nonsense. You look fine," her mother waved a hand at her clothes and winced. "How often do you go out to eat?"

Molly thought back to the last time and couldn't remember.

"Exactly," her mother's lips pressed together. "Take Parker to that cute little Italian place. They have great food, and if you get anything on your shirt, it won't matter anyway."

"Because it's dirty," Molly said, her tone flat. "That's what I get for crawling up hillsides after a wreck."

"Oh, sweetie." Her mother frowned. "If you're not feeling well, just stay here. I can have the doctor look you over again."

"No, I'm fine," Molly said. "But Parker might not want to go out with me."

"I know the place you're talking about." Parker grabbed her hand and waved his other hand at her mother. "We'll be back in an hour and a half."

Molly's mother chuckled. "I do so like a man who takes charge. You two enjoy."

Parker led her out of the room again, nodded to Boomer and told him their plans. Then he hurried her to the elevator, down to the parking lot, and they drove out to the street in his truck.

"Are you on a mission or what?" Molly asked.

"Yes. I'm hungry and didn't want to stand around arguing with you in front of your mother."

"You see what she was doing, don't you?" Molly asked.

"Trying to set us up on a date?" Parker nodded. "I saw that. So?"

"You didn't have to go along with her."

"What if I wanted to?" he asked.

"You could have asked the nurse at the nurses' station to go with you," Molly said, refusing to glance in his direction. "She's much prettier, and she likes flirting with you."

"I didn't want to go to dinner with her. I don't know her."

"You could get to know her," Molly insisted.

"I don't want to get to know her. I want to have dinner with you. Can we stop talking about the nurse at the nurse's station? Otherwise, I'll think you were jealous," he said, giving her a pointed glare.

Molly sputtered. "Jealous. As if!"

Out of the corner of her eye, she could see the smile on Parker's face. The louse. He was enjoying teasing her.

Nevertheless, Molly's heart swelled, and heat suffused her body. Parker Bailey actually wanted to take her out to dinner. Dirt and all.

She pulled the visor down and gasped at the swaths of dust on her cheeks. "I can't go to a nice restaurant looking like this."

"You look fine. But if you're that concerned, here." He pulled a napkin out of the console between them and handed it to her.

She wiped at the dirt, removing the majority of it. Then she ran her fingers through her hair, trying without succeeding to tame the wild curls she usually kept secured in a ponytail. "It's hopeless," she said, and slumped against the seat.

"I love it like that," Parker said. "It's kind of wild and untamed...like you."

"I'm not wild and untamed," she said.

"Compared to your father, you are." He winked. "I like that about you."

"I'm not wild." She hid the smile that threatened to emerge. "My hair *is* untamed, though."

"Here we are. Saliano's," he said, pulling into the parking lot.

"You know this place?"

Parker nodded. "I eat here once a month. I know

the owner and his wife."

"You eat here once a month?" Molly frowned. "How is it I didn't know this about you?"

He shifted into park and opened his door. "You never asked."

Before she could climb down on her own, he was there, pulling open her door for her. He held out his hand.

Molly placed hers in his and let him help her down from his truck.

"I know," he said. "you don't need help."

"Yeah, yeah," Molly said. "Your mama trained you better."

"That's right." He grinned and opened yet another door for her.

She liked that he teased and treated her like a lady. Who knew Molly McKinnon would go all girly? "I need to be careful, or I might get used to this."

"Count on it."

No. She couldn't let that happen. Guys like Parker didn't fall in love with girls like her.

As soon as Parker stepped through the door of Saliano's, a cheer went up from the wait staff and the owners.

"Parker! *Benvenuto, amici miei!*" a man called out from behind the counter. He came around it and enveloped Parker in a bear hug that crushed Parker's ribs.

"Massimo, it's good to see you."

A woman's cry sounded from behind a swinging door. A moment later, a small, rounded woman with salt and pepper hair rushed out. "Parker, *benvenuto, amore mio!*" Once again, he was enveloped in a bear hug that took his breath away.

When at last the woman released him, she stood back and studied him. "You've lost weight."

Parker laughed. "It's nice to see you, too, Bianca."

"Are you staying with us tonight?" Massimo asked. "Your room is ready."

Parker shook his head. "Not tonight. I'm just here for dinner." He stepped back and brought Molly forward. "Massimo and Bianca Saliano, this is Molly McKinnon from Eagle Rock."

Bianca stood back, her gaze raking Molly from head to toe. "She's too thin. What are they feeding you at the Iron Horse Ranch?" She shot Parker a stern look. "Are you Parker's *fidanzata?*"

Molly looked from Parker to Massimo and back to Bianca. "I don't know what that means."

"Girlfriend," one of the pretty waitresses said as she passed by Molly.

Molly's eyes widened. "Oh, no. We're just friends."

Bianca frowned. "You are a girl. You are Parker's friend?"

Molly nodded. "Yes."

Bianca nodded. *"Fidanzata."* The woman wrapped her arms around Molly and hugged her so tight Molly's eyes bugged.

When Bianca was done hugging, she kissed Molly on both cheeks. Then Massimo treated her to the same.

By the time all the hugging and kissing was done, Molly's cheeks were pink, and she was breathless.

"Benvenuta, Molly." Bianca waved a hand toward a table near the windows. "Come, have a seat."

Throughout the meal, Bianca and Massimo did what the Italian couple did best...they showered Parker and Molly with love, attention and all the Italian food they could possibly eat. With the pasta, they poured glass after glass of wine until Parker held up a hand. "Please, no more. I have to drive."

Molly laughed and smiled as the flamboyant couple argued, kissed and argued over every little thing, but they always came back to Parker and Molly with smiles.

When the meal was over, Bianca and Massimo tried to convince Parker and Molly to stay the night.

"I can't," Molly said. "My mother's in the hospital. I'm staying with her tonight."

Bianca's eyes widened. *"Perdonami.* I did not know. Wait." Bianca disappeared into the kitchen. Minutes later, she reappeared with an aluminum tray covered in foil. *"Per tua madre.* For your mother."

Molly hugged the woman and then Massimo.

"Thank you for such a wonderful meal and making me feel like family."

"Oh, but you are *famiglia*," Massimo said. "You are Parker's *fidanzata*."

Molly smiled, and Parker led her out of the building and helped her into the truck.

Once they were on the road back to the hospital, Molly turned to him and said, "What just happened back there?"

He chuckled. "What do you mean?"

"I feel like I was just adopted by the Salianos."

Parker laughed out loud. "That's exactly what happened to me when I came to Montana looking for a job and a place to live. I stopped for a bite to eat, they fed me, invited me to stay, and ever since, I'm like their long-lost son." His smile persisted. "I come here once a month and stay with them, help out in the kitchen and become one of the *famiglia*."

Molly sat back in her seat, shaking her head, a smile pulling at her lips. "I like them."

"I'm glad you do. They can be a little over-whelming, but they mean well and love uncondi-tionally."

Back at the hospital, they found Boomer in Mrs. M's room, playing a hand of poker.

"We brought a gift from the Salianos." Parker set the plate the family had sent on Mrs. M's rolling tray table.

"Thank goodness, you two are back. This woman

just beat me in ten hands of poker. I think I owe her two hundred dollars."

"Oh, don't be silly. We weren't playing for real money," Mrs. M said. "If we had been, I would've raised the stakes." She winked. "Thank you, Boomer, for entertaining me."

"No, thank you, Mrs. McKinnon. I've never played poker with such a formidable card shark." He winked. "If you need anything, I'll be outside."

Boomer left the room.

The flirty nurse arrived to take Mrs. M's vitals. She left and came back with two blankets. "For you two, since you're staying the night."

Parker took the offering, thanked the nurse and handed one of the blankets to Molly. After the nurse left the room, Parker leaned close to Molly's ear and whispered, "Not interested in her."

The warmth of his breath on her neck made Molly's insides ignite. She took the bench by the window.

Parker stretched out in the lounge chair.

"Thank you for being here with me," Mrs. M said, her voice fading to a whisper. "I miss James."

"We do too, Mom," Molly said softly. "He'll be back."

"I hope you're right," Mrs. M said.

Parker lay for a long time, listening to the sounds of movement in the hall outside the room, thinking about the Salianos, Molly and the McKinnons. He'd gravitated toward the Salianos and the McKinnons because of what he'd been missing in his life.

Family.

He prayed they would find Mr. McKinnon soon. For Molly's sake. For Mrs. M's and for all the McKinnons. They loved the man and were lucky to be a part of the Iron Horse Legacy.

Tomorrow, they had to come up with something new, something different to help them find Mr. McKinnon. The family couldn't hold out much longer before someone broke.

CHAPTER 8

"Mom's home!" Molly called out as she helped her mother through the door into the big house and into the living room. "Sit."

"Really, Molls," she said. "I can walk on my own. They cut off the good drugs at midnight. I'm perfectly sober."

"Mom..." Angus hurried forward with Bree beside him.

"Mrs. McKinnon...Mom," Bree said, "I'm so glad you're home. We've all been worried."

"I'm fine. The night in the hospital was just a precaution. Other than a sore rib and a bump on my head, I'm as good as new."

"Mom," Colin came in too. "Good. You're home." He hurried forward and hugged her gently.

Still, she flinched. "Careful. That particular rib is broken."

"Like I said," Molly reminded her, "sit."

"Okay." Her mother frowned. "When did you get so bossy?"

"When you didn't listen to what the doctor told you. You're to rest and relax to give that rib a chance to heal. That doesn't mean for an hour. He meant several days."

"Oh, that's ridiculous. I'm fine but for a little twinge." She twisted just a little and cringed. "Okay, I'll sit, but I plan on cooking dinner."

"No, you aren't." Emily entered from the hallway to the kitchen. "I have a crockpot going with a huge roast, potatoes and carrots, and I made fresh bread rolls. It'll all be ready around dinnertime."

"Emily, honey, thank you so much."

"And Fiona made an apple pie," Emily said.

As if on cue Fiona entered the living room, carrying Caity. The baby squealed when she saw Molly's mother and held out her arms.

"Sorry, sweetie." Duncan scooped his daughter up in his arms. "Grandma can't hold you for a few days."

Distracted by her new favorite person, Caity batted at her daddy's head and giggled when he blinked.

"That's so not fair. I want to hold my grandchild," Molly's mother said.

"And you will, when that rib has had a chance to mend." Molly helped ease her mother into a lounge chair and kissed the top of her head. "You'll be okay. Just give yourself time."

"Here's the mail to keep you busy for a few minutes," Jenna said, handing the injured woman a stack of envelopes and a letter opener.

"At least, I can be useful for something."

Molly smothered a grin. "Mom, you're not a very good patient."

"You mean I'm not a very patient patient," she said with a grin. "I crack myself up." She stuck the letter opener in an envelope and ripped it open. "Don't mind me, I'll just be ripping and reading while you all are getting on with your lives."

"Mom, you're too much," Bastian said and leaned down to kiss the top of her head. "You're not bruised there are you?"

"No, sweetheart." She gave him a weak smile. "I do appreciate all of you. I'm just not used to sitting while everyone else is working."

"Just pretend you're the queen, and we're all your subjects. Your wish is our command." Bastian bowed low.

"Now, you're just getting on my nerves." His mother shook her head. "Get out of here. Go mend a fence or break a horse." She chuckled. "Queen. That will be the day."

"Mom, you have a visitor," Angus said.

Molly's mother turned her head as far as she could without twisting her body. "Who is it?"

"Miss Hannah, it's me, Earl Monson." The old mountain man had become a fixture at the Iron Horse Ranch since he'd helped Bastian and Jenna find the bastards who'd tortured James McKinnon.

"Earl, honey, please come in. Caity will be so glad to see you."

Earl took a seat beside Molly's mother, and then sank to the floor.

Duncan placed Caity in the old man's lap.

The baby giggled and pulled at Earl's beard, making the old man laugh.

Parker touched Molly's arm. "While your mother is entertained, let's go check on the animals in the barn."

She nodded and slipped out of the room while the rest of the family milled around her mother. She was glad to be home where everything was familiar and work made her feel good about life.

She and Parker walked to the barn where the horses were still in their stalls, instead of out in the field where they could graze.

Molly and Parker got busy feeding horses, cleaning hooves and brushing the tangles out of their manes and tails. One by one, they turned the horses loose in the pasture and went back to work on the next.

At one point, they were both in the tack room at the same time. The room barely had space for them to turn around. It was crowded with saddles, blankets and bridles, as well as the equipment they needed to clean hooves, worm cows and generally take care of a place as big as the Iron Horse Ranch.

Molly started to back out of the room.

"Wait," Parker said. "You have a piece of straw in your hair." He moved closer and plucked the offending straw loose. His gaze caught hers and held.

Molly's heartbeat sped, and she swayed automatically toward Parker.

He cupped her cheek and leaned forward, capturing her lips with his. "I've wanted to do that all day," he said.

She laughed, a little breathlessly. "Then why didn't you?"

"I was waiting for the right time."

"And waiting until I had straw in my hair and dirt under my fingernails was the right time?" she whispered, her breath lodged halfway up her throat.

"Yup. That's sounds about right." He smiled and kissed her again, gathering her as close as he could in the tight space.

A barn door creaked open and closed.

"Molly?" Bastian's voice sounded. "Are you burning trash somewhere?"

Molly jerked away from Parker and stepped out of the tack room. "No. Why?"

Parker came out after her.

"I smelled smoke." Bastian looked from Molly to Parker. "Did I interrupt something?"

"No." Molly's face burned. She stepped past Bastian and headed for the barn door, hoping Bastian would follow and forget that he'd seen her and Parker come out of the tack room. "From which direction did you smell the smoke?"

"I thought it was coming from the direction of the barn. That's why I asked if you were burning something."

The three of them stepped out of the barn and rounded the building to look behind.

Smoke rose from the far end of the hay field.

Molly's heart dropped to her knees. "Grass fire."

"Go to the house, call 911 and notify the fire department," Bastian said. "We need everyone out here now."

Molly ran for the house, her heart pounding, fear rising up into her throat.

She burst through the back door, yelling, "Grass fire. Call 911. Need all hands on deck outside with buckets, wet towels, old blankets. Anything we can use to put out the fire." She ran into the living room. "Not you, Mom. You and Fiona need to stay with Caity. If it gets bad, you need to get into the truck and head to the highway."

"I can help," her mother said, struggling to rise from the lounge chair.

"No, Mom," Molly insisted. "I'll have Hank Patterson's man, Kujo, spray water on the house and barn in case the fire gets close. He'll be out there to protect you, Fiona and Caity. Please, don't try to help. We'll spend more time worrying about you than worrying about the fire."

"Okay. Fiona, get my gun out of the drawer beside my bed. If anything happens, we need to be ready."

Fiona left Caity in Earl's care and ran up the stairs to Molly's mother's room. She was back in less than a minute with the gun and a magazine of bullets.

Earl pushed to his feet and handed Caity to Fiona. "I'll help with the fire."

"Earl, are you sure?" Molly's mother looked up at the old man.

"A grass fire needs every able-bodied man and woman to help stomp it out." He nodded and left the room.

Molly pointed a finger at her mother. "Stay away from the fire."

Her mother's lips twisted. "You really have become bossy."

Molly frowned. "If I could trust you to behave, I wouldn't have to be so bossy."

"Now, who's the child?" Her mother jerked her head toward the door. "Go. You're needed outside more than in here. I'll call 911."

Molly raced for the linen closet and grabbed all the oldest towels. On her way back through the kitchen, she snagged the handle of the mop bucket and a broom. Then she ran out of the house, passing Earl on her way toward the barn.

Already, Kujo had a garden hose out, spraying water on the roof of the house. His dog, Six, moved with him, pacing near his feet, as if the smell of smoke made him nervous.

Molly stopped long enough to scoop water into the bucket from the water trough. She dunked all the towels into the water and flung them over her shoulder. Armed with wet towels and a bucket of water she half-walked, half-ran across the field.

Her brothers, Taz, Jenna, Bree and Emily were halfway to the line of fire, carrying buckets of water, shovels and brooms.

If they could get to the fire quickly enough, they might have a chance to stop it from spreading.

Molly hurried as fast as she could without sloshing all the water from the bucket.

Smoke rose from the burning grass, blowing toward them, which meant the fire was moving their direction.

Molly caught up with the others and handed out wet towels to everyone.

Wrapping a small towel around her mouth and nose, Molly took a larger one and attacked the line of fire, beating it with the towel. When the towel dried too much, she ran back to her bucket and soaked it. When the bucket was empty, she took up the broom she'd brought and used it to pound the flames.

Soon, they were joined by the volunteer firefighters out of Eagle Rock. They took over with a tanker truck and a pumper truck, spraying water at the flames.

Everyone else fought the falling embers that would start new fires ahead of the line.

Working alongside Earl, Molly lost sight of Parker in the smoke. Her eyes and her lungs burned, but she couldn't stop for fear the fire would eventually reach the house where her mother, Fiona and Caity were.

A four-wheeler burst through the flames and smoke, heading directly for Molly.

She didn't see it until it was almost on her.

Parker, from a few steps away, yelled, "Molly! Get down!"

Molly dropped to the ground.

Parker raised his handgun and fired at the moving target. His shot missed, and the rider kept coming. The man pulled a gun from beneath his jacket and aimed at Parker.

Beside her, Earl Monson lifted his broom and swung it at the rider, letting loose.

The rider fired at Parker at the same time as the broom hit the rider, bumping his hand as he pulled the trigger. The bullet missed Parker and slammed into Earl. The old man dropped to his knees, pressing a hand to his gut.

Parker got off a shot, hitting the rider in the shoulder. The impact made him jerk the handlebar of the ATV, sending it into a spin that threw him off.

He staggered to his feet, holding onto his arm. One of the volunteer firefighters aimed the water hose at the man, knocking him off his feet.

Parker raced forward and pinned the man to the ground.

Molly stayed with Earl, applying pressure to the wound in his belly. "Stay with me, Mr. Monson. The ambulance will be here soon."

"Wouldn't bother me none if I died," he said. "I'd be with my wife again."

"You're not going to die, Mr. Monson. There's a little girl at the house who loves pulling on your beard. She would be very sad if you didn't come to visit."

Earl smiled up at her, though his brow was creased in pain. "That Caity-did is going to be a heartbreaker someday."

"It would be a shame if you didn't stick around to see that day," Molly said. "Stay with me, Mr. Monson."

"You're a good girl, Molly McKinnon. Your daddy must be proud of you."

The firefighters and all the volunteers soon had the blaze contained.

The sheriff arrived at the same time as the ambulance. Two EMTs worked to stabilize Earl Monson and loaded him first. A third medical technician, under the surveillance of the sheriff and his deputy, worked on the ATV rider. The sheriff read the man his rights as the EMTs loaded him into a second ambulance.

After the ambulance left with one of the sheriff's deputies escorting him, the sheriff found Angus.

Molly joined her brothers.

"The man on the ATV is Mark Janson, a local thug. He said he was paid five hundred dollars to start the fire and snag the redhead when everyone was too busy to notice. They told him it would be easy. Two-fifty up front. Two-fifty when he brought her to the junction of Bear Claw and Dry Creek Roads. I have a unit heading to that location as we speak."

"If the guy who hired him has access to a police scanner, he won't be there."

The sheriff nodded. "I thought of that. Fortunately, I had just enough reception on my cellphone. I called my deputy on his cell. It's not being broadcast over the scanner."

"Let us know what you find," Angus said. "Did Janson say who hired him?"

"No, just that he was approached by a man wearing a dark hat outside the bar on the edge of Eagle Rock. He had his hat pulled down low and stood in the shadows. He didn't say who he was, just offered him money. Janson took it with the promise of more where that came from, if he delivered the girl." The sheriff's lips twisted. "Mark was worried about what would happen if the man he shot died. He swore he'd tell us everything he knew if we didn't charge him with murder."

"If Earl Monson dies," Molly said through gritted teeth, "Mark Janson better pay for what he did."

The sheriff nodded. "I promised nothing. At the very least, Janson will be charged with attempted murder and arson. He'll spend time in jail."

Parker slipped an arm around Molly. "I owe the old man. If he hadn't thrown his broom at Janson, it could have been me wearing a bullet. Earl saved my life."

Molly shook her head. "And to think he's lived years isolated in the mountains over the loss of his wife. He's a good man. I'm glad he's no longer hiding away. And Caity loves him." She looked down at her hands, which were covered in Earl's blood. "I hope he makes it."

"You did good by applying pressure to his wound. If the bullet didn't hit any vital organs, he should be okay," the sheriff said.

"If." Molly sighed. "Have you found out anything else about my father's disappearance?"

The sheriff shook his head. "Sadly, no."

Molly never felt so tired as she did at that moment. "I'm going to get a shower," she said.

Parker kept his arm around her waist as they walked back to the house, gathering singed towels and brooms as they went.

Parker dumped them in the burn barrel when they passed it and kept moving with Molly.

Inside the house, Fiona paced with Caity.

Molly's mother still sat in the lounge chair, her worry showing in the deepened lines around her eyes. "Did they get the fire put out?"

Molly nodded. She didn't want to tell her mother about the second attempt to kidnap her, but she needed to know about Earl.

"Someone came after me while everyone was working the flames."

Her mother gasped. "Oh, baby. I should've been out there with you."

Molly shook her head. "I had plenty of protection. Parker shot at the man driving the ATV. When the man pulled a gun and shot back, Earl Monson flung a broom at him, knocking his aim off. Unfortunately, the bullet hit Earl."

"Oh, dear Lord," her mother cried. "Is he…"

"He was still alive when the EMTs loaded him into the ambulance."

Her mother buried her face in her hands and cried. "Why is this happening to us and the people we care about?"

Molly knelt beside her mother and held her hand. "We'll get through this."

"Yes, we will," her mother said and looked up, her gaze capturing Molly's, "but will Earl? Will your father?"

"They have to. We've gone through too much. They've sacrificed too much," Molly's fist clenched. "Damn it, we'll all pull through."

"I pray we do," her mother said. "I pray we do."

CHAPTER 9

WHILE MOLLY WAS in the shower, Parker went to Angus on the back porch. "I'm not the right man for the job of protecting Molly."

"What do you mean?" Angus's brow furrowed. "You're the only man for the job. You've been there all three times she's been attacked and saved her from the men trying to take her."

"I'm always a little too late."

"Not the way I see it," Angus said. "If you were a little too late, she'd have been taken a lot sooner."

"Still, I don't think I'm the right man for the job."

"Do you have someone else in mind?" Angus challenged him.

Parker hadn't thought of alternatives. He felt like a failure after the last two attempts they'd made to get to Molly. But the thought of relinquishing his responsibility left him feeling anxious and scared for the woman he'd come to care about.

"No," he said. "I don't have someone else in mind."

"I can hire one of Hank's guys to protect her," Angus offered. "Is that really what you want me to do?"

Parker turned and paced away from Angus and stopped to look out over the charred pasture.

If he hadn't been with Molly following her into town, the person driving the SUV could have pulled her or her mother from the truck and taken off with them.

If Parker hadn't been there when the two ATV riders had made that first attempt to grab her, they would have taken her then.

This last attempt had gotten Earl Monson shot. Parker hadn't been close enough to Molly during the fire, but he'd been there to shoot at the guy and keep him from taking her.

He couldn't let someone else take over the job of protecting her. He wouldn't be able to breathe not knowing what was going on. "No," he said, looking down at this hands. "I want to be the one to look out for her."

Angus's eyes narrowed. "Are you falling in love with my little sister?"

Parker's head jerked up. "I'm the foreman. Your sister is the boss's daughter."

Angus chuckled. "You didn't answer my question. Are you in love with Molly?"

Parker drew in a deep breath and let it out slowly. "Yes."

"Then you're the right man for the job," Angus said, as if that was the only answer. "Just curious... how long have you known?"

Parker shook his head. "I think I've been in love with her since I started working here. I just wouldn't let myself admit it." He looked up at Angus. "She's the boss's daughter. I have no business being in love with her."

"Why the hell not?" Angus asked.

"I respect your father. I wouldn't do anything to hurt him or any one of the McKinnon family."

"And you think loving Molly will hurt a member of my family?" Angus snorted. "You're messed up, you know that?"

Parker shoved a hand through his sooty hair. "I know I'm messed up. I love your sister so much I can't see straight anymore."

Angus cocked an eyebrow. "I guess the big question is, does she love you?"

"I don't know," Parker said. "There's something between us. I know I love her, but is that *something* love on her part?" He shrugged. "I don't know."

"Why don't you ask her?" Angus said. "I've learned that if you want something bad enough you have to be willing to fight for it. For her. No matter what."

Parker nodded. "You're right. I won't know if she cares for me like I care for her, unless I ask her."

"Then what are you waiting for?"

His lips twisted. "The right time?"

"No time like the present." Angus grinned. "Go ask her."

"What if she doesn't love me?" Parker paced the length of the porch and back.

"Then I can hire someone else to protect her," Angus said.

"No," Parker said. "Even if she doesn't love me, I wouldn't feel comfortable letting someone else take on the responsibility of keeping her safe."

"Sounds like you've got it bad." Angus clapped a hand on his shoulder. "If it means anything to you, I approve of you two being together. You're a good man, Parker. My sister could do worse."

"Thanks. I think." Parker laughed. "I hope she doesn't have to do worse than me."

Angus glanced toward the house. "I need to get Bree back to her place. The animals there need to be tended." He held out his hand.

Parker shook it. "Thanks for letting me bend your ear."

"Anytime. Hopefully, we'll be calling you brother, soon." Angus winked. "Don't wait too long to ask. You'll want to begin the rest of your lives as soon as possible."

"Huh?"

Angus chuckled. "Together. You'll want to begin the rest of your lives together as soon as possible." He shook his head. "Amateur. I take it you've never been in love before?"

Parker shook his head. "No."

"Well, good luck," he said. "You're gonna need it. My sister can be hardheaded. But when she loves someone, she's all in."

As he stood on the porch, Parker watched the sunset, waiting for Molly to get out of the shower so that he could get in. He didn't want to corner her for an answer when he smelled like smoke and sweat.

The sound of Molly's voice brought him back to the task at hand. She was out of the shower. It was his turn to clean up. Then he'd ask her.

He hoped the words would come to him while he stood under the spray. They sure hadn't come to him watching the sunset.

"Mom, what are you doing?" Molly entered the living room in time to see her mother struggling to get out of her lounge chair.

"I'm tired of sitting," her mother said, wincing when she twisted just a little. "I need to move and do something before I go out of my mind."

"At least, let one of us help you out of that chair." Molly hurried forward, took her mother's arm and helped her to stand. "The broken rib has got to be hurting you."

"It is," her mother said, straightening slowly.

"Want me to get you one of the pain pills your doctor prescribed?" Molly retained her hold on her mother's arm until she was steady on her feet.

"No. I don't want to become addicted to them and end up overdosing because I'm an addict."

Molly laughed. "You? Never. You're one of the toughest women I know."

"Damn right, I am." She batted away Molly's hands. "A little pain won't hurt me. It's a good reminder to be thankful."

"Thankful?"

"Yes, thankful." Her mother cupped her cheek and smiled. "Every day I wake to see my children and grandchild is a day to be thankful for."

Molly chuckled. "I get your point and love your attitude. And you're right." She stepped away, watching to make sure her mother could walk without support.

The woman shuffled slowly but steadily out of the living room, carrying the mail she'd opened.

"Where are you headed now?" Molly asked, following her mother.

"To the kitchen," she responded.

"Not to cook," Molly said, her tone stern.

"Fine. I won't cook, but I think I can make myself a cup of tea."

"I can do that for you," Molly said. "Why don't you have a seat at the table while I get the pot boiling?"

Her mother stopped, blocking the entrance to the kitchen. "What part of I can make myself a cup of tea did you misunderstand?"

Molly held up her hands. "Okay. You can make your own tea."

"Thank you," her mother said with a thick layer of sarcasm. She handed her half the stack of mail. "You can throw those away for me."

"What about the rest?" Molly asked as she carried the torn envelopes and advertisements to the garbage pail.

"I need to do something with these. Some are bills that need to be paid. And there's an invitation to the Lucky Lady Lodge for a fundraiser to help save the lodge. I need to RSVP to that."

Molly's head jerked up. "You're not going, are you?"

Her mother's brows dipped. "Of course, I am. I refuse to stand by and watch the places that were such a big part of my life shrivel up and die, especially when I can do something about it. Your father would go with me, if he were here. He knows how I feel about the lodge."

"What's the big deal about the lodge?" Molly asked. "Why are you so interested in its success?"

Her mother smiled with a faraway look. "I worked there as a waitress at the restaurant and helped the cleaning staff when they were over-whelmed with the summer crowd." She sighed. "I loved that place. It had so much history in its walls. They say there are secret rooms and passages all through the old lodge. I never found them, but rumor had it there was one in the library. I think I moved every book on the shelves, opened every cabinet and felt along all the wood panels for knobs, buttons or switches and never found anything that looked like it could trigger a hidden door to open."

"But can't you just donate some money? You don't have to actually go to the lodge for the fundraiser."

Her mother nodded. "I know. But I need to get out. I haven't gone anywhere since your father disap-peared until my trip to the hospital." She frowned. "That doesn't count."

"But the lodge will be filled with people."

"Most of whom we will know," her mother noted.

"I'm sure Lewis Griffith will invite past customers as well. It could be crawling with people we don't know. What if one of them is the person holding Dad hostage?"

Her mother's face firmed into tight lines. "All the more reason to go then. We can set ourselves up as targets with plenty of bodyguards intermixed. When someone makes a move to grab one of us, we'll catch him, and he'll lead us to your father." Her face bright-ened. "The more I think about it, the more I like the idea."

Molly poured boiling water into a mug holding a teabag and carried it over to the table. "I don't like the idea of putting you in danger. You almost died."

"Don't be silly. I'm fine. Nothing that won't mend."

"Yeah, but if the guys holding Dad want to make him talk, they could put a whole lot of hurt on one of us to make it happen."

"Did you hear the part about having plenty of bodyguards in the mix?" She took the proffered mug and stirred in a teaspoon of sugar and a little cream.

"The idea makes me very nervous," Molly said. "What if they cause a distraction like they did with the fire? If everyone is running in different directions, the bodyguards might lose track of one of us. They could swoop in and take you, me...even one of the boys. You saw how they tried to drug me. What if they slipped a roofie into one of our drinks?" Molly shook her head. "No. We can't risk your life."

Her mother's mouth firmed. "It's my life. If I want to risk it, I will. I'm tired of waiting for some clue to emerge. Weeks have passed, and your father is still not home. I know he'd risk his life for me. Why not risk my life for him? You'd do it for Parker, wouldn't you?"

Molly had been on the verge of arguing the point with her mother when the woman had brought up Parker. For a second, she froze. Yes, she'd risk her life for Parker. Her mother wanted to do the same for the love of her life.

Her mother reached across the table and touched Molly's hand. "You love Parker, don't you?"

Molly nodded. "I do."

"If he were in the same situation as your father, you'd do anything to get him back, wouldn't you?"

Again, Molly nodded. "But...you're my mother. I can't let you do this."

"You can't stop me, either." She straightened her shoulders.

Molly pointed to her mother's side. "You have a broken rib. If they capture you, they'll use your weakness to cause you more pain."

"I'm tired, Molly. Tired of the chase, the mystery, the not knowing. Mostly, I'm tired of lying down at night in my comfortable bed without my husband, while he's probably lying on a cold, hard floor or in the dirt, hungry, hurting and close to death." She placed both hands on the table. "We're McKinnons. We're going to war to take back what belongs to us."

Molly nodded. "Okay. We're going to a party. I hope everything turns out all right. I don't want to lose both my parents."

Her mother pushed to her feet, wincing.

"Where are you going?" Molly asked.

"To call Hank Patterson. We'll need the help of his Brotherhood Protectors."

Molly didn't try to stop her. When her mother got

a thought in her head, she was like a pit bull with a stick between her teeth. She was going through with this insane idea whether the rest of the family liked it or not.

Parker chose that moment to walk through the door, his hair wet from his shower, freshly shaved and smelling like his aftershave. His brow twisted as he glanced back down the hallway. "Why is your mother calling Hank Patterson?"

Molly shook her head. "Get ready for a rough ride."

He turned and smiled at her, making her stomach flipflop. "What do you mean?"

"Mom's on the warpath. She's declaring war on Dad's captors."

"Does she know something we don't?"

Molly sighed. "No, but she's over all of this waiting. If we can't find the people who are holding my father, we can make it easy for them to find us."

Parker frowned. "I don't like the sound of that."

"Neither do I, but I'm beginning to lean in her direction."

"What exactly does she have planned?"

"Not much, other than putting herself up as bait to flush out the bad guys."

"No way." Parker shook his head. "You have to talk her out of it. She's in no shape to handle what they'll have in store for her."

"You know that. I know that." She jerked her head

toward the hallway where her mother was talking to Hank on the land line. "Try telling her that."

"What are we going to do?" Parker asked. "We can't let her go through with it."

"We're going to call an intervention."

"You'll need your brothers," Parker noted. "When does she plan to make this happen?"

"At the Lucky Lady Lodge fundraiser," Molly said. "That gives us just a day to find my father or come up with a plan to keep from losing both our parents."

CHAPTER 10

THE NEXT MORNING, Parker stood in the Brotherhood Protectors' war room in the basement of Hank Patterson and Sadie McClain's house on the White Oak Ranch. Hank, Taz, Kujo and Boomer were there well before the McKinnon clan arrived.

Molly, her four brothers, their significant others and their mother had gathered around a large white board on the wall where a timeline depicted the dates of the ex-convict's escape, his subsequent death, their father's disappearance, finding the ring James always wore, finding the house where he was tortured and the men who'd performed the torture, and finally, the attacks on Molly and her mother.

"They're getting desperate if they've made three attempts in as many days," Hank said.

"That's why I wanted to take this opportunity to be more proactive," Mrs. M said. "The fundraiser will expose us to everyone in the community and have enough people there for our bad guys to mix and mingle with us under the radar."

Parker hid a smile at Mrs. M's tone. She sounded like a general describing her battle strategy.

"Whoever is in charge of this effort has to be someone in the community," Swede said as he entered the room carrying several gold chains with shiny pendants dangling from the ends.

"Which means, we probably know who it is," Mrs. M said. "It breaks my heart to think anyone I know could be so evil as to torture a neighbor, all for the love of money."

"They can't even spend it, because it's marked," Parker said, shaking his head.

"That's what the layers of corporations and off-shore companies are for," Swede said. "Once they find the money, it'll be laundered all around the world. It'll get spent somewhere."

"I wish we could find that money and use it to bargain for our father's release," Colin said. "Has anyone tried to get inside William Reed's demented head?"

"Kind of hard to do when he's dead," Molly muttered.

"Yeah, I know," Colin said. "Has anyone talked to the people he knew and hung out with? Were there any places he frequented?"

"The man was in the mountains when he was shot. He was probably looking for the money then."

"Or meeting with the person who helped him escape," Swede said. "I did a search of all his known addresses prior to his arrest for the murder of the driver and guard and the theft of the money from the armored car.

"We sent out some of our guys to question Reed's friends, girlfriends and former roommates. None of them had contact with him during the months prior to the heist."

Hank picked up the story. "Reed's ex-girlfriend said he spent more and more time in the Eagle Rock area. He told her he was fishing. She thought he was sleeping with another woman. He finally dumped her and didn't even bother to come get his stuff from her trailer. She threw all his stuff out in the yard. When he still didn't come to collect it, she burned everything."

"That's too bad," Bastian said. "There might've been some record of where he'd spent his time and with whom."

"Did he have any credit cards? A cellphone we could trace?"

Swede shook his head. "Nothing. He must have used a burner phone and cash. Someone had to have helped him with the heist and the escape. The *who* is where we're stumped."

Hank took the necklaces from Swede. "From now until we recover Mr. McKinnon, we need to be able to track all the women. Any one of you could be their next target." He went around to all the ladies. "These necklaces should be worn at all times. You can even wear them in the shower. They're waterproof, and they'll allow us to track you should you be separated from the family."

Swede went around the room with small metal disks, handing them to the men. "Put one of these in a pocket or your shoe. Have it on you whenever you leave the house."

"How will we know whose is whose?" Angus asked.

"Whoever is not where he should be will be the one we'll be looking for. Otherwise, we could spend a couple of hours assigning codes to each of them."

"No, thanks," Molly said, slipping the necklace over her head. "We still have a ranch to run."

"The fundraiser is tomorrow evening at the Lucky Lady Lodge," Swede said. "Each of you will be assigned a buddy to stay with at all times. The members of the Brotherhood Protectors will keep track of each pair and provide backup if something goes amiss."

Swede pulled up a rough schematic of the lodge and displayed it on a large monitor to the right of the white board. "The event will start in the dining room where those people who purchased the limited number of plates will eat. Once dinner is over, everyone will move to the ballroom where more guests will join you in the ballroom."

"Me and my men are getting into the event with ballroom tickets," Hank said. "They'll be waiting for you in the ballroom, having gone around the room, planting miniature web cams in both the ballroom and the hallway leading to the bathrooms."

"I'll keep an eye on you from those webcams and the GPS devices. The Brotherhood Protectors and prior military McKinnons will be equipped with communication devices in the form of earbuds. You'll check in when you arrive in the ballroom. And if there is anything out of the ordinary, say something."

"We know the people we're up against have weapons. If there is any gunfire, don't stand around looking at each other," Hank said. "Hit the ground." He nodded to the men who'd all experienced combat. Then he gave a narrow-eyed look at the women. "Everyone hits the ground. Do you understand?"

Molly nodded along with her mother, Fiona, Emily, Jenna and Bree.

"In the meantime," Hank said, "don't say anything to anyone about the money, the fundraiser and our plan."

"Everyone on board with this?" Angus asked. "Me, personally, I'd rather the ladies stayed home."

All six women shook their heads.

"As for Caity," Hank continued, "she'll be here with Chuck Johnson, Sadie and Emma. Sadie would be coming to the event, except she's getting pretty close to her due date and doesn't want to risk hurting herself or the baby. So, she'll stay with Chuck and the little ones. Boomer's wife, Daphne, will be here with their little girl Maya to help out."

"Until then, we go about our lives, business as usual, keeping close to your buddy," Angus said. "They might make an attempt again today. Be ever mindful."

Parker approached Swede. "Have you found anything else about the corporation that paid Otis Ferguson to torture Mr. McKinnon?"

Swede nodded. "Not enough to take to the bank yet, but there is a connection to a mining company I thought interesting. Only I can't find the bank associated with the company or if the company is currently a going concern. I'm sifting through hundreds of mining companies. Most of those with an online presence are current or recently defunct. None of them are the Lettie's Lucky Strike Mining Company or LLSMC. I've combed through every angle I could. I'm not finding anything."

Mrs. M's eyes narrowed. "Isn't there a historical registry of mining companies in this area at the library in Eagle Rock?"

"I believe so," Jenna said. "I had to research a particular mine on a county plat for a client once. The records were all on microfiche. They haven't had the time to convert them to digital."

"Wow," Mrs. M said. "I haven't looked at microfiche in decades."

"What's microfiche?" Bree asked.

Jenna chuckled. "I asked the same thing when the librarian led me to the historical records. It's an archaic, plastic film you insert into a microfiche reader that enlarges the images so that you can read them. I can run by the library later this afternoon. I have to show a property in an hour, otherwise I'd go straight there."

"Parker and I can check into it on our way back to the ranch," Molly volunteered. "The animals are good to go until this evening. We have the time," her gaze met Parker's, "right?"

He nodded, just as interested in finding the Lettie's Lucky Strike Mining Company. If it led them to the owner and the person holding Mr. McKinnon hostage, he was all for looking through old records.

"It can be tedious," Jenna warned. "Don't expect great results right out of the chute."

Parker didn't care. Any action was better than no action with regard to finding his boss.

. . .

THE FAMILY LEFT the White Oak Ranch, some heading back home, others making their way to Eagle Rock. Duncan loaded his mother, Fiona and Caity into his truck. Colin and Emily would follow them to make sure they made it back safely.

Parker held the door of his truck open for Molly to climb inside. She didn't even make a comment about how she could do it for herself.

He smiled.

She was getting used to having him do things for her. And he didn't seem to mind doing them.

That was a good sign. Right? Or was he this nice to all women?

Molly was falling more and more hopelessly in love with the man. She found herself wanting to say the words and watch his reaction. But she was afraid. She figured it wasn't a good time to drop that on him. Not when her mother was making plans to use herself as bait to flush out the bad guys. They all had more important things on their minds.

They followed Bastian and Jenna back to Eagle Rock, stopping at the library on Main Street.

The building wasn't very big and had been donated to the city so long ago no one would've remembered who'd donated it, except for the fact it had a plaque on the sidewalk naming the long-ago donor.

Inside the library, the air smelled of books, paper

and that musty scent only an old building could produce.

The librarian was excited to see them and glad to show them the microfiche drawers and how to use the reader. Soon, they were sifting through county records with images of documents signed back in the late 1800s when the gold rush changed the west.

They started with the L's and worked their way through hundreds of claims and mining records.

Molly worked with one of the microfiche readers, while Parker worked the other. When they got through all of the Ls and hadn't found that particular name, Molly went back to the front desk and asked the librarian about women named Lettie who'd lived or died in the county.

The librarian showed her how to search through the birth and death certificates of people who'd been born or died in the area from the 1840s until the present.

"Who are you looking for?" the librarian asked. "Anyone in particular?"

"All we have is the name Lettie."

The librarian frowned. "Lettie was short for Charlotte back in the late 1800s, on into the early 1900s. You might want to look for Charlotte."

"Thank you," Molly said, and hurried back to Parker. "Pull out the Cs. We might be looking for the wrong owner. Lettie is short for Charlotte."

They found the microfiche films from the Cs and combed through them, finding a couple mining companies named Charlotte. They looked up the longitude and latitude of those. One was located closer to Bozeman than Eagle Rock.

Another was located just outside of Eagle Rock.

Parker whistled.

"What?" Molly asked. "What did you find?"

"When I key the coordinates of the Charlotte's Lucky Strike Mine into the computer, the location comes up on the same mountain where the Lucky Lady Lodge stands."

"That doesn't make sense. The Lucky Lady has been there for as long as I remember," Molly said. "I've never seen any mining operations conducted anywhere on that mountain. I can ask my mother. She worked at the lodge."

"Would be worth a look," Parker said. "We can swing by on our way to the Iron Horse Ranch."

"Let's do it." Molly stood and started to clean up the microfiche films.

"The librarian said to leave the films. She'll put then back where they belong. We need to get to the mountain with plenty of time before the sun sets."

Molly's brow wrinkled as she looked at her watch. "Wow, we've been here for hours."

"Jenna warned us," he reminded her.

"Yes, she did. We need to hurry. The sun sets

soon, and we won't see much if we get there after dusk." She led the way to the truck and waited while Parker opened her door for her. Her arm brushed against his chest, setting off a firestorm of sensations inside her. "What is it about you that makes me all shaky inside?" she said without thinking. As soon as the words were out of her mouth, she clapped a hand over her lips. "I didn't mean to say that out loud."

He chuckled and leaned into her. "I'm glad you did, because I was feeling it, too." Then he kissed her, cupping the back of her head with his hand.

Molly melted into the man, her hands rising up to circle the back of his neck. She opened to him, her tongue sweeping out to connect with his in a long, slow glide. The rest of the world around them faded away in that kiss, until someone cleared her throat.

Molly looked over her shoulder at the librarian standing on the steps of the library. "You forgot your notepad," she said, her cheeks pink.

Molly stepped away from Parker and retrieved the notepad from the flustered woman. "Thank you." Then she let Parker hand her up into the truck. She didn't say a word as they drove toward the mountain and the Lucky Lady Lodge.

As they neared the turnoff to the lodge, Parker didn't slow. He shot a glance her way. "I thought we'd look around the mountain. Maybe we'll see something on one of the back roads." He passed the lodge road and continued along the road located at the base of the mountain. Pavement turned to gravel as they climbed the side of the hill, moving in and out of the trees, traversing switchbacks and areas where the road had partially washed out. About halfway up the side of the mountain Molly spotted a dark spot above them. "There," she said pointing to it. "Is that a cave or a mine entrance?"

Parker slowed the truck and rolled down his window. "Hard to tell. The road is getting a little too narrow for my truck. It'd be better if we were on ATVs."

Molly looked at him, her eyes narrowed. "Whoever has been attacking me has access to at least four ATVs. Perfect for these kinds of trails." She looked ahead. "There's a flat spot ahead where you can turn your truck around while we still have plenty of light. We can get out and climb the rest of the way."

His brow wrinkled. "It's a pretty steep grade."

She grinned. "Afraid you can't make it?"

"As a matter of fact, climbing is hard on my bum leg. But I can make it, if you can"

"I can do it." She frowned. "I keep forgetting you had a war injury. We can take it slow getting up there, but I want to see what it is."

"Agreed." He pulled up to the flat spot and eased his truck around in the tight space, aiming it downhill for when they returned.

Parker dropped down from the truck. Before he

could get around to her side, Molly was out and met him at the front.

Together, they climbed the hill. In areas, they stuck with the trail. Sometimes, they went straight up to cut the time it would take to walk the switchbacks. As they neared the dark entrance, Molly could see timbers framing the opening.

"It's a mine shaft," she said.

The wood beams bracing the entrance were weathered but appeared to be solid.

She pointed to an image at the top center. "Is that an eagle carved into that crossbeam?"

Parker studied the image. "Looks like a flying eagle."

"Seems like a lot of work for a mine air shaft." Molly shrugged. "Are we going in?"

"Let me go first," Parker said. "I'm armed."

Molly nodded and waited below. Parker pulled his gun out of the holster beneath his jacket and climbed up to the opening. A moment later, he holstered his weapon and waved for her to join him.

Molly scrambled up the hill.

"It's been sealed. Someone probably used a stick of dynamite to blow the entrance to keep people from going in and getting lost in the shaft."

"So there was a mine in this mountain," she said.

"*Was.*"

"Wasn't it pretty standard to have air vents in the shafts?" Molly asked. "Could this have been one?"

Parker shrugged. "I'm not a mining expert, but I think you're right."

Molly looked up at the sky. "We don't have time to explore further today. But we should let the others know there was a mine here. Maybe since we found it under another name, Swede will have more luck looking for it online."

"Right. But for now, we need to get down before it gets too dark to see."

Going down proved a little harder than going up. The gravel was slippery, and many times Parker had to catch her before she slid off the edge of a drop-off. By the time they reached the truck, the sun had sunk below the highest ridge, throwing the mountainside into dusky shadows.

Parker drove slowly and carefully back down the rutted mining trail until they emerged onto the graded gravel road and, finally, back to pavement.

"So, what does it mean that we found an old mine on the mountain?" Molly asked, looking to Parker in the light from the dash.

"I don't know. It could mean nothing, or it could be yet another clue to lead us to who paid Otis Ferguson to do what he did to your father."

Molly pulled out her cellphone. "Now that I have reception, I'm calling Hank. He can get Swede to do his magic with the internet. Hopefully, our day at the library wasn't a waste of time."

"Hey, Molly," Hank answered. "Did you find anything in the historical records at the library?"

"Not for Lettie's Lucky Strike Mine, but we did find Charlotte's Lucky Strike Mine. The recorded location is on the same mountain where the Lucky Lady Lodge is located."

"Interesting," Hank said. "I'll get Swede on that name ASAP."

"We drove up the back side of the mountain on some old tracks and found a blocked mine entrance."

"Blocked?"

"Yes, as in someone probably used a stick of dynamite to seal the shaft to keep people out."

"There are a lot of mines and shafts in the Crazy Mountains. Some of them have been sealed, others are still open," Hank said. "You didn't run into anyone out there did you?"

"No," Molly said. We made it back down without interference."

"What was the condition of the road up there?"

"Barely wide enough for the truck and not all the way up. It appeared to have been abandoned. I doubt it's been used in a while."

"I'll see if I can get a drone up there tomorrow. Kujo's fiancée has one we can use. I'll see if she can get it out there before the fundraiser."

"Thanks, Hank...for all you and your team are doing for my family," Molly said.

"I wish we were farther along than we are," Hank

said. "Your father should be home enjoying his granddaughter by now."

"He will be soon." Molly ended the call and swallowed hard on the lump in her throat.

Parker reached for her hand and held it all the way through Eagle Rock and back to the Iron Horse Ranch.

Molly had never considered herself a needy female. She prided herself on her independence. But right at that moment, she was glad to lean on Parker's strength. He made her believe things would turn out all right.

They arrived at the house after dinner had been served and the kitchen had been cleaned.

Emily met them at the door with a smile. "Colin and Bastian took care of the animals. I left two plates full of food warming in the oven. Eat, grab a beer and join us on the back porch."

"How's Mom?" Molly asked.

Emily gave her a crooked grin as she led them to the kitchen. "She went to bed early, determined to be at her best tomorrow, despite her broken rib."

"Sounds like Mom."

"We're all worried about her. None of us want her to go to the fundraiser tomorrow," Emily said.

Molly sighed. "When she's on a roll, there's no stopping Mom. Hopefully, with Hank's men, these GPS trackers and all of us there, we'll keep her safe."

"I hope so. We all love her so much." Emily

nodded toward Parker. "Don't forget to grab that beer and join us on the porch." She left them to their own devices, grabbed a couple bottles of beer and left through the back door.

Parker pulled the plates out of the oven and set them on the kitchen table while Molly filled glasses with tea. They ate in silence, listening to the low hum of voices out on the porch.

When they finished, they worked side by side to wash up and dry the dishes.

Molly retrieved two long neck beers from the refrigerator, popped off the tops and handed one to Parker.

When they emerged onto the porch, her brothers and their ladies were spread out in rocking chairs on the porch swing and sitting on the steps.

"We were just talking about you two," Bastian said.

Molly's cheeks heated. "What about us?"

"We're going to a party tomorrow night," Colin said.

"So?"

"What are you going to wear?" Angus asked.

Molly shrugged. "I don't know. I haven't given it much thought."

"It's semi-formal. You'll need a dress," Colin said.

Bastian chuckled. "Do you even own a dress?"

Molly's cheeks filled with heat. "I think so."

156

Although the last time she'd worn a dress had been when she'd graduated high school.

"Don't let your brothers be such assholes," Bree said.

"That's right," Jenna interjected. "You'll have a dress. We'll make sure you do."

"I don't want to be a bother, and if things go south, the dress might be ruined," Molly started.

Fiona shook her head. "Don't you worry about it. I think I have just the dress for you. Our coloring is similar."

"But you're a head taller than I am."

"I know, but I have the perfect cocktail length dress that will fit you to the floor. Afraid I won't be able to loan you the shoes. Your feet are much smaller than mine."

Emily placed her foot beside Molly's. "I have a pair of shoes you can wear. I think we're close enough in size."

"What about you, Parker?" Angus asked.

"I have a suit I bought for a friend's funeral that I can wear."

Bastian clapped his hands. "Then we're all set for the big event."

Molly perched on the porch rail beside Parker. "Do you really think this is going to work?"

"It has to," Angus said. "Mom is counting on it."

"And everyone is ready for this to end," Colin said.

"And for Dad to come home," Duncan added, balancing Caity on his knee.

"I'm scared for Mom," Molly said.

"We all are," Jenna said.

"And we'll all be careful to watch over her," Angus said. "If we could talk her out of going, we would."

Bastian snorted. "That's not going to happen."

"Then we'll all have to keep vigilant and take care of each other," Duncan hugged Caity close. "Good thing Chuck will be watching out for Caity. He's the best."

Molly drank her beer, the alcohol taking the edge off her anxiety about the next night and the possibility of pushing their problems to a head.

Parker slipped his arm around her waist and held her close. When he finished his beer, he took her empty bottle from her hand. "I'm headed in for a shower."

"I'm tired. I think I'll call it a night as well." She hugged her brothers and kissed Caity. "Good night."

As Molly walked up the stairs beside Parker, he reached for her hand. The mellow feeling she'd gotten from the beer rapidly changed into a heat that spread through her chest and lower into her belly.

When they stopped in front of her bedroom door, Parker pulled her into his arms. "What is it about you that makes me all shaky inside?"

"I'm feeling it, too," she whispered back.

Then his mouth crashed down on hers.

She reached behind her, twisted the knob on her door, shoved it open and stepped inside. With her other hand curled into his T-shirt, she dragged him across the threshold, never losing contact with his mouth.

The kiss went on long enough she forgot when the last time was that she'd taken a breath. Was this really happening?

CHAPTER 11

BLOOD BURNED through his veins and down to his groin. This woman...sweet Jesus... this woman was everything he needed and more.

He slipped his hand beneath her shirt, loving the feel of her smooth, soft skin beneath his fingers.

Molly leaned back, a smile spilling across her face. "Grab your things and meet me in the bathroom." She turned him around and pushed him back through the doorway.

Parker hurried to his temporary bedroom, snagged clean shorts and his toiletries kit and was across the hall less than a minute later.

Molly appeared shortly after, carrying a thin robe and nothing else.

Parker's heart skipped several beats as their gazes met. "Are we doing this?"

"If by this, you mean getting a shower?" She

nodded, strode past him into the bathroom and turned, cocking an eyebrow. "Are you coming?"

Parker dove through the door and closed it, twisting the lock behind him.

Molly smiled. "You know, this will be my first time taking a shower with someone else."

"Are you sure you want this? Because it's all a little weird to me, being in the boss's house about to take a shower with his daughter."

Her brow twisted. "Can you, for one minute, forget I'm the boss's daughter?"

"I don't know." Parker wondered if he'd regret things in the morning. "I have a lot of respect for Mr. McKinnon."

"I love my father, but I'm not thinking about him at this moment." She reached for the hem of her shirt and dragged it up over her head, tossing it into the laundry basket in the corner. "It would be really weird for you to think about him right now." Gripping the button on her waistband, she flicked it open. "Who are you thinking of now?"

He cleared his throat. "You and how much I want to hold you in my arms." Parker peeled his shirt over his head and tossed it into the laundry basket with hers. He reached for her, brushed aside her fingers and lowered the zipper on her jeans. "I want to feel your body against mine. With nothing between us."

"Now, you're sounding like you mean it." She

flicked the button loose on his jeans and slowly slid the zipper down.

Parker groaned and slipped his fingers into the waistband of her jeans to cup her bottom with his palms. "Do you know what you do to me?"

She smiled and pressed her hips to his, her belly rubbing against his erection. "I have a pretty good idea."

The next few seconds were spent stripping down to the skin. When they stood in front of each other naked, Parker's heart was pounding, and his breathing was ragged.

"Wait," he said and reached into the back pocket of his jeans, extracting his wallet. Sweet Jesus, he hoped he had protection. When his fingers curled around a couple of foil packets, he almost let out a yelp of relief.

He laid the packets on the counter, reached into the shower and turned the knob, setting the spray to a comfortable heat. Then he bent, sliding his hands over her bottom and down to grasp the backs of her thighs, and then lifted her.

Molly wrapped her legs around his waist and pressed her breasts against his chest.

Parker stepped into the shower and turned her so that the water ran down her back, over her shoulders, and dripped off the tips of her breasts. He lowered his head to capture one of her nipples between his teeth.

Molly moaned, her back arched and her breast surged into his mouth.

He flicked the tight bead with the tip of his tongue and swirled it around in his mouth.

His groin tightened, and his cock hardened. He wanted to be inside her, but he wanted to please her first.

Tasting the other nipple, he flicked and toyed with it until her fingers slipped through his hair and pulled gently.

"Please," she said.

He chuckled. "Please what?"

"More, please," she said.

Instead of teasing her nipples, he lowered her to her feet and lathered a bar of soap in his hands. With great care to touch every part of her body, he smoothed soap across her skin, over her shoulders, the mounds of her breasts and lower. His fingers slid over her ribs, along the curve of her waist and down to the juncture of her thighs.

Molly captured his hand and pressed it over her sex. With her other hand, she gripped him in her palm and ran her fingers over the length of him.

Parker thrust into her grip. "You tempt me."

"I hope I more than tempt you," she whispered and raised her mouth for his kiss.

He pressed his lips to hers, pushing his tongue past her teeth to taste hers. She was soft, yielding and more beautiful than he could have imagined. Under the tough cowgirl exterior was a soft, curvy woman who fit him perfectly.

She took the soap from him and lathered her hands. Then she ran them over his entire body, taking her sweet time, making him so hard and so desperate to be inside her, he could hardly breathe.

He stepped beneath the shower head, bringing her with him. When all the soap was rinsed away, he started his own exploration of her body with his mouth, kissing a path from her lips down her neck to first one, then the other breast.

He wanted to take his time, but his body urged him to move it along, go a little faster, and get to the business of pleasing this woman. He dropped to his knees, water running over his head and shoulders as he kissed her belly and down to the tuft of hair over her sex.

With his thumbs, he parted her folds and touched her there with his tongue.

Molly moaned. Her fingers, buried in his hair, kneaded his scalp in frenetic circles. "Parker," she said. "I can't."

"Can't?"

"Can't wait. Please, I want you inside me."

"Not yet. You're not there."

"I'm so close," she whispered.

He flicked her clit with the tip of his tongue.

Molly's body jerked, her hips thrusting toward him.

He flicked her again, his hands cupping the backs of her thighs to bring her closer.

Her muscles tightened in his grip, and her body stiffened.

Parker flicked again, swirling his tongue around that little strip of flesh, until she threw back her head and her fingers dug into his scalp. "Parker," she cried softly.

When she finally drew a breath, he released her and straightened to his full height. The water was cooling on his back. He turned it off, reached for a towel and dried her quickly.

"Please, tell me it's not over," she said, her voice strained.

"I hope not," he said and handed her a dry towel.

She dried him, taking her time to carefully dry him down there. When she was done, he slipped into his shorts and wrapped her robe around her beautiful body. Snagging the foil packets from the counter, he unlocked the door.

A quick peek out into the hallway, and he turned to her. "All clear. Your room or mine?"

She smiled. "Mine. Your room is my brother Angus's. No. Not happening there."

He grinned, took her hand and hurried across the hall.

Once they were inside her room, he closed the door, turned the lock and tugged the robe from her body. He slipped out of his shorts, lifted her into his arms and carried her to the bed in the center of the room.

He carefully laid her on the mattress and crawled up onto the bed between her legs.

She parted her knees, bringing them up, her heels pressing into the comforter.

Parker tossed one of the packets onto the pillow beside her and tore open the other with his teeth.

She extracted the condom and rolled it down his shaft, and then positioned him at her entrance. "Now," she said. "All the way. I need you to fill me all the way."

He nudged her slick entrance, testing how tight she was. When he slid into her, he did so a little at a time.

Molly grabbed his ass and slammed him home.

Parker sucked in a breath and held it, buried deep inside her tightness, his cock rejoicing, encased in her heat.

Then he moved, sliding almost all the way out.

She pulled him back in, setting the pace, moving his hips faster and faster until he took control and pumped in and out, harder and harder.

Her feet dug into the mattress as she lifted up to meet him thrust for thrust. Then her body went rigid, and she dug her fingernails into his buttocks. Her eyes squeezed shut, her breathing ragged. "Yessss."

Parker shot to the stars. He pushed deep inside her and held still as his shaft pulsed his release.

When at last his body relaxed, he sank down on top of her and lay for a moment before rolling to the side, taking her with him.

Molly pressed her lips to his chest. "That was amazing."

"Yes, it was," he said, just getting his breath back.

"Can we do it again?" she asked flicking her tongue over his nipple.

He laughed. "Right now?"

"It doesn't have to be right now. I just don't want it to be the last time."

He gathered her close in his arms and held her to him. "I don't want it to be the last either."

"I do believe I might be feeling the L word for you."

Parker laughed. "Lust."

"Definitely that," she said and sucked at his nipple. "No, the other four-letter L word."

Something loosened inside Parker. If she was saying what he thought she was saying, she loved him.

"I'm feeling that L word for you, as well." He smoothed his hand over her riotous red hair, the damp wave curling around his fingers. "Definitely the lust word and the other four-letter L word."

"Mmm. I like that." She yawned and snuggled close. "Will you still respect me tomorrow?"

"Even more so, Molly. Even more so." He kissed her forehead and settled into his pillow.

Parker was exactly where he wanted to be. Lying naked with this woman who was brave, yet vulnerable, strong, yet gentle and more beautiful in her natural state than any beauty pageant winner.

He hoped that their effort to flush out Mr. McKinnon's captor didn't go south. If all went well and they got Mr. McKinnon back alive, he wanted to tell Molly what L word he was feeling for her. Then he'd take an even riskier step and ask her father for his daughter's hand in marriage.

A lot was riding on the fundraiser for the Lucky Lady Lodge. He hoped it worked out the way they planned. And if they did manage to tempt the snake out of the grass, that he would be easy to identify and take down. More than that, he hoped they'd find Mr. McKinnon and bring him home alive.

CHAPTER 12

"THE GUYS ARE GOING to flip when they see you," Fiona said.

Emily's smile was so wide, Molly thought her face was going to split. "I can't believe it's you."

Bree grinned. "Fiona, that dress…"

"I know, it's perfect on her." Fiona hugged Molly. "If you want it, it's yours. I never looked that good in it."

Jenna sighed. "You're like…I can't even describe it."

"Cinderella?" Molly said as she stared at her reflection in the mirror. The pale green gown complemented her auburn hair. The shimmery fabric fit her body like a second skin, following every curve and the swell of her breasts and hips like it was made for her. "I feel like my fairy godmother used her magic wand on me." She frowned at herself. "Is that really me?"

"It is. And you're beautiful," her mother said from the door.

Molly turned.

Her mother wore a long white gown that set off her beautiful salt and pepper hair and green eyes, which were so much like Molly's.

"Oh, Mom," Molly hugged her gently. "Dad always loved that dress on you."

"I hope he gets to see it tonight when we find him." She handed Molly the necklace Hank had given her with the simple gold pendant. "Will you? I shortened the chain so that it would lay better on my neckline."

Molly hooked the latch at the back of her mother's neck and stood back. "I don't know how you do it. I just hope that when I'm your age I look as good as you."

"You're stunning. You're going to shock your brothers and take the breath away from your young man."

Emily fussed with Molly's hair that she'd affixed to the back of her head in a loose, messy bun that looked natural yet elegant. "So, are you and Parker officially a thing?"

Jenna clapped her hands. "Please, say yes. You two are perfect together."

Molly shrugged. "I don't know."

"Has he told you he loves you?" Fiona asked.

Molly thought about what they'd said to each other the night before after making love. He hadn't actually said it outright. Did it count? "No. Not yet."

"That boy needs to get on it. A girl needs to know where she stands," Bree said.

"It'll happen," her mother said. She took her daughter's hand. "You can see it in his eyes. He loves you."

"And you can see it in Molly's eyes that she loves him." Jenna sighed. "I love a good romance."

"Me, too," Emily said.

"Are we ready, ladies?" Molly's mother asked. "Everyone have on their jewelry?"

All five young women nodded, fingering the necklaces Swede had given them.

"Then let's go find the bastard who turned our lives upside down." Molly's mother marched from the room, looking elegant and deadly.

"Stay back," Jenna said to Molly. "Let us all go down first, and then make your entrance. I want to see their faces when the guys see you."

Molly frowned but hung back while the others descended to the bottom of the staircase where the men waited in the foyer.

When they were all on the ground floor, Molly sucked in a fortifying breath and started down the stairs, one step at a time, concentrating on not falling in the pretty silver heels Emily had loaned her.

"Holy shit," Bastian called out. "Is that you, Molls?"

"What happened to our little sister?" Colin asked Emily. "Was she your science experiment?"

Emily grinned. "She looks amazing, doesn't she? I did her hair."

"Amazing barely expresses it," Duncan said, holding Caity in his arms. "You look good, Molly."

Molly heard all of what her brothers were saying, but Parker was the only person she saw.

He stood there in a black suit with a black tie and a crisp white shirt. His hair was slicked back and his chin clean-shaven. He was so handsome he took her breath away.

Parker's eyes flared when he saw her, and he followed her progress all the way down the stairs, moving to meet her at the bottom. "Molly."

"Parker."

"Have you two met?" Bastian teased.

Molly nodded her head. "We have."

"Good, because we need to get going." Bastian opened the front door and held it for everyone as they left the house.

Three trucks lined the drive, clean and sparkling.

"We're riding with Angus and Bree," Parker said. "Colin and Emily are riding with Bastian and Jenna."

"Who are you riding with, Mom?" Molly asked.

"I'm riding with Duncan, Fiona and Caity. We're going by Hank's to drop off Caity with Chuck,

Sadie and Daphne. We'll meet up with you at the lodge."

Molly frowned. "Are you sure you'll be okay?"

Her mother nodded. "We'll be fine. Kujo is meeting us at the gate and will follow us to Hank's. All of Hank's guys will escort us to the lodge."

Molly smiled. "Good. You can't have too many bodyguards."

"True," her mother said. "Now, go. It's going to be an eventful night."

Parker cupped her elbow, led her out to Angus's truck and settled her into the back seat.

Soon, they were on the road to the Lucky Lady Lodge, where they hoped to lure the bad guys out into the open.

She scooted close to Parker, drawing on his strength for what might come later. Molly hoped the night didn't end in tragedy. It was time for the McKinnons to claim a happily ever after.

She loved that she looked good in the dress Fiona had loaned her, and the look on Parker's face when he'd seen her coming down the steps had been worth the primping and the gallon of hairspray Emily had applied to tame her curls. But if shit hit the fan, Molly would rather have been wearing jeans and her worn but comfortable cowboy boots. A good pair of boots could provide a lot more protection than a flimsy set of high heels.

Molly pushed back her shoulders and lifted her

chin. No matter what she was wearing, if anyone tried to hurt her family, she was going to kick some serious ass.

PARKER WISHED he'd driven his own vehicle. Sitting in the back seat of Angus's truck made him anxious. Behind the wheel of his own truck, at least he felt like he had some control over the situation.

Going into the Lucky Lady Lodge this night was like walking into a pit full of rattlesnakes. He felt certain someone would strike, but he didn't know who. The uncertainty had his gut in a knot and his fists permanently clenched.

Having Molly sitting beside him didn't make the situation any better. She'd been attacked three times. Would tonight be the attackers' lucky night? Would they finally succeed in capturing Molly or her mother? And if they did, would the McKinnon clan and Hank's team get to her fast enough to save her life?

If Parker had been driving his own truck, he would be turning around and taking Molly back to the ranch where he could keep her safe.

All too soon, they arrived at the front entrance of the lodge. Angus stopped long enough to let his passengers out of the vehicle. Then he drove around to park the truck.

Parker stood with Bree and Molly until Angus rejoined them.

As they stepped into the lodge lobby, they were greeted by Lewis Griffith and his wife, Traci.

"Welcome to the Lucky Lady Lodge," Lewis boomed. "You don't know how delighted I am that the entire McKinnon family bought tickets to the dinner and the ball. Thank you. Your donations to the lodge will help to keep the old place in business."

Traci held out her hand to Angus. "Angus, glad you could make it to the fundraiser. Every donation counts toward keeping this old place functioning and up to code."

"Thank you for inviting us," Angus said. "We're always glad to help the community and local businesses. I'm curious, though. I thought the Lucky Lady was doing well. It always seems to have a crowd during the summer."

Lewis sighed. "We've been here a long time. Expenses continue to rise, what with having to bring old electrical and plumbing systems into the new century. But we've kept our prices steady, encouraging people to return year after year. It covers the daily operating expenses, but not the upgrades."

"I hope this event gets the funds you need to make those upgrades."

"Me too, or we'll be forced to close and sell."

"Oh, we're not selling," Traci said. "We'll find another way to keep the place, but we're not selling."

Lewis smiled at his wife. "For someone who didn't like the lodge and the history it stands for, my wife has done a complete about face about the place. She's the one who suggested the fundraiser and did all the marketing and soliciting for donations from individuals and local businesses." He slipped his arm around his wife's waist. "She's amazing when she sets her mind to do something." The lodge owner looked past Angus and Molly. "Where's your mother? I thought she was coming."

"She'll be here soon enough."

"Is it too soon for her to be out after the car accident?" Lewis asked.

"Wild horses couldn't keep her away," Angus replied.

Colin and Bastian arrived and joined the crowd gathering around Lewis and his wife.

Angus, Bree, Parker and Molly entered the lodge and stood in the lobby where members of the community greeted each other like long lost friends, not people they saw every day.

Molly introduced Parker to the owner of the diner, Jenna's boss, the head of her real estate firm and one of the local lawyers. He wouldn't remember their names by the end of the evening, and he didn't really care. He was with Molly and she was his only concern for the night.

By the time they'd made their rounds through the room, shaking hands with more people than Parker had interacted with in a year, Molly's mother arrived with Duncan and Fiona.

"Comm check," Hank's voice came into the earbud Parker wore. Swede had equipped all the men with communications devices, since they were the ones carrying weapons beneath their jackets.

"Parker here," he responded.

One by one each man checked in.

A person dressed as a chef tapped a knife against a crystal goblet and announced that dinner was served.

The dinner guests were escorted to the second floor dining room where place cards identified who was sitting where.

The McKinnons were spread out all over the vast dining room. At least, the couples were assigned to the same table.

Mrs. M. was the odd man out, assigned to a table near the front and far enough away from her children that Parker wasn't happy.

Molly wasn't pleased either, if her frown was any indication. "I don't like that she's so far away from any of us."

"Please, take your seat," Lewis Griffith said, speaking into a microphone. "The Lucky Lady's chef has created a wonderful meal for your pleasure tonight. Please...enjoy."

Waitstaff carried huge trays of covered plates, laying them out on the tables in front of the guests.

Molly sat sideways in her seat, her gaze on her mother.

Parker also sat sideways, watching the older McKinnon for any sign of trouble.

The meal progressed without incident.

When the plates were taken away empty, the guests rose and followed the waitstaff assigned to guide the guests to their next entertainment, the ballroom, where a live band was just finishing a warmup.

The shuffle from the dining room had Parker on edge. He lost sight of Mrs. M for four entire seconds. His body tightened, preparing itself to bash through the crowd to get to her before she was abducted and taken to wherever they were holding Mr. McKinnon.

"Do you see my mother?" Molly asked, her fingers digging into his arm. "I can't see her."

"I saw her a moment ago," Parker said as he craned his neck to see over the throng of people crowding through the double doors of the ballroom.

A gap formed between people, big enough for Parker to catch a glimpse of Mrs. M smiling and chatting with someone inside the ballroom. She spotted him and Molly, and gave them a short, tight wave.

Parker escorted Molly into the ballroom and took her straight to her mother. As the two hugged, Parker scanned the room, making a mental note of where each of Hank's men were positioned. They were spread evenly around the area and close to exits.

Their presence only made Parker feel marginally more secure. All it would take for chaos to reign was one tug on the fire alarm, and everyone would rush for the exits, making it impossible to sort out the McKinnons in the commotion.

The band played a combination of tunes from the 1940s, soft rock and roll and some country and western ballads.

Couples crowded the dance floor, smiling and laughing as if nothing was wrong, no one would be harmed, and the evening was nothing more than what it was advertised to be.

Parker's lips twisted. For all he knew, the evening would end with nothing awful happening. They'd go back to the ranch, he would make love to Molly and they'd sleep soundly in each other's arms.

Wishful thinking didn't always come true.

Mrs. Griffith made her way around the room, smiling and thanking the guests for coming out to support the lodge. When she stopped in front of Molly and Parker, she thanked them, too. "Is there anything I can get for you?" she asked.

Molly grimaced. "Is there a ladies' room nearby? I'm afraid I drank too much water at dinner. Which, by the way, was wonderful. Please, thank the chef for us."

Mrs. Griffith smiled. "I will. If you want to follow me, I'll show you to the ladies' room." She turned and started to walk away.

Molly touched the woman's arm. "Oh, please, don't let me bother you. If you could tell me which way to go, I can find it myself."

"Nonsense," she said with a dismissive wave. "It won't take any time at all." She took Molly's hand and shot a smile at Parker. "We'll be back shortly."

Parker followed them all the way to the entrance of the ladies' restroom and stopped right outside the door. He didn't like that Molly was out of his sight, even for a minute. But what could go wrong in a ladies' restroom?

He must have been frowning hard. A couple of women came out of the bathroom, took one look at him and hurried past.

As he was waiting, his cellphone vibrated inside his pocket. He pulled it out and recognized Swede's number. "Bailey here."

"Parker, I found something interesting. Can you talk?"

"Yeah," Parker said. "Shoot."

"I found an old drawing of the Charlotte's Lucky Strike Mine. There are tunnels all over the inside of that mountain. But get this, the lodge was built over the main entrance."

Parker sucked in a harsh breath. "Are you certain about that?"

"If these schematics are accurate, the mine entrance is somewhere beneath the Lucky Lady Lodge."

"How can that be?"

"They didn't have building codes back when they constructed that lodge. The owners of the mine thought the gold veins had played out. They sold the land to a wealthy man who built the lodge over the mine entrance. The lodge has been passed down from generation to generation since it was built."

"So, Lewis Griffith is the latest generation to own the lodge and the mine beneath it?"

"No. Not Lewis."

"Then who?" Parker asked, knowing the answer before Swede said it.

"Traci Griffith," Swede said. "She's the great, great, great granddaughter of Charlotte Pendergast, the woman who purchased the mountain and the old mine and built the lodge. Rumor had it that she supplemented the lodge's income with gold dust from the mine."

The more Swede talked, the tighter the knot squeezed in Parker's gut. "I've got to go. Call Hank. Let him know what you learned. Traci Griffith just showed Molly into the ladies' room. I'm going in to make sure she's all right. Standby to locate Molly. I'm not sure, but my gut says she could be in trouble."

MOLLY HAD ENTERED THE LADIES' room with Mrs. Griffith and had gone straight to one of the stalls. Other women were just finishing up and washing their hands with a running commentary about the dresses other women had worn to the event.

When Molly had finished and washed her hands, Mrs. Griffith appeared behind her. "I understand your mother used to work here at the lodge."

Molly smiled. "Yes, she did, probably back before you were born."

"Would you like to see some of the secret passages?"

"I'd love to, but I'd need to bring Parker with me. I hate to leave him standing out there alone."

Mrs. Griffith gave her a knowing glance. "Afraid some woman will steal him away?"

"Actually, yes." Molly laughed. "He's so handsome. I'm not quite sure what he sees in me."

"I wouldn't worry too much. You're a beautiful woman." She raised her arm and patted Molly on the shoulder.

"Thank you," Molly said. A sharp sting on the back of her neck made her flinch. "What the—"

"Did you just feel something sting the back of your neck?" the other woman asked, a concerned frown denting her brow.

Molly reached up to feel where her neck still hurt from the sting. "Yes. I did."

"We have a problem with stinging bugs in the lodge. I can apply some medicine to the sting, if you'll follow me to the medicine cabinet over here against the wall."

"Parker…" Molly said, her tongue not really cooperating, her vision blurring as well as her thoughts. "What did you say?"

"Over here. I can give you something to make you feel better." Mrs. Griffith took her arm and led her toward what looked like a cabinet door in the middle of the wall.

The woman opened the door, but the cabinet was empty. In fact, the floor of the cabinet was lower than the door by a couple feet.

"Do you see anything in here that will help?" Traci smiled and stood back, while tugging on Molly's arm, edging her closer to the open cabinet.

Her head swam, and she felt like going to sleep right there…standing up…

"Go ahead, get in. I'll show you one of the secret passages," the lady was saying. She gave Molly a hard shove.

Molly's hips caught the edge of the cabinet door. She doubled over, her feet coming off the ground.

Another shove from behind flipped her over the edge, and she landed in the bottom of the cabinet on her head. Her head spun so fast she couldn't tell what was up or down. She felt the earth move, and suddenly, she was falling, falling, falling until the cabinet came to a jolting halt and the lights blinked out.

CHAPTER 13

PARKER PUSHED the door to the ladies' room, expecting it to swing open. When it didn't, he pushed harder.

Damn. Traci must have locked it from the inside.

Parker backed to the wall outside the ladies' room, tucked his shoulder and ran full tilt into the door. The frame splintered, but the lock held, and his shoulder throbbed. He cocked his good leg and kicked the door hard, close to the lock. The frame split, and the door swung inward, slamming against the wall.

Parker ran in to find an empty room. Just to make sure, he pushed the doors open to all the stalls.

No Traci Griffith. No Molly. Nobody.

"Guys," he said into his communications device, "we have a problem."

"What's wrong?" Angus responded immediately.

His throat clenched, and anger, guilt and despair burned hot in his chest. "Molly's gone."

"What the hell happened?" Bastian demanded.

"It's Traci Griffith. She showed Molly to the bathroom, and they both disappeared."

"My mother always swore there were secret passageways in that lodge," Angus said. "Did you look around?"

"I'm doing that now." Parker walked along the walls, touching the wallpaper, looking for secret doors. He came to what appeared to be a picture frame. When he touched it, it moved. Not like a frame tilting sideways, but like a door he could open. He pulled it toward him, discovering what appeared to be a very large, deep cabinet. A cabinet that could fit a person. When he reached inside and pressed his hand to the bottom, the entire cabinet structure dipped slightly.

"I think I found how she got Molly out of the bathroom."

"We're on the way," Angus said.

"Fiona, Taz and I will stay with Mom," Duncan reported.

"Good luck holding her back," Bastian's voice spoke into Parker's ear.

"Not telling her anything until we know more," Duncan said.

"Good," Angus said.

A moment later, Angus, Colin, Bastian and Hank

burst into the ladies' restroom and came to stand beside Parker.

"Looks like an old fashioned dumbwaiter," Hank said. He leaned inside and pulled on something. The box shifted downward.

"I'm going in," Parker said and started to climb into the box.

Hank gripped his arm. "That's what they'll expect you to do."

"Yeah, man," Bastian said. "You'll be a sitting duck when the door opens on the other end."

"Can't have my future brother-in-law dead before he says I do," Angus said.

Parker pulled his leg back out of the dumbwaiter. "I can't stand here twiddling my thumbs. They have Molly." His cellphone vibrated in his pocket.

Swede.

"They got Molly," he said, before Swede had a chance to say anything. "You found a schematic of the mine. Is there one for the lodge? One that shows all the secret passages?"

"As a matter of fact, that was why I was calling. I found it on the dark web. It shows the secret passages inside the architectural structure of the building, but I'm not sure how easy it will be to find them. Some of them could have been walled over. Others might be behind bookcases, stairs or other pantry walls. If they took her into the mountain, the GPS tracker might suffer diminished reliability."

"There's a ladies' restroom off the north end of the ballroom. Traci Griffith got Molly out through a dumbwaiter in the restroom. Where does it go, and what passages lead to and from the dumbwaiter?"

"The lower level of the lodge is where the laundry facility is." Swede paused. "There aren't any secret passages from that level, but there are some on the first floor.

Angus jerked a thumb toward Colin. "We'll check out the laundry room."

"That dumbwaiter stops on the first floor in a hallway. No hidden passages on the hallway, but there appears to be one off the library and a room labeled 'sitting room'. These drawings might be from when they first built the lodge in the early 1900s. The rooms may have been reconfigured."

Parker didn't wait for all the information. "Swede, stay on the line. I'm heading to the library."

"I'm going with you," Hank said.

"I'll take the sitting room." Bastian said.

"Do you have something belonging to Molly?" Hank asked as he ran after Parker. "An item of clothing, a hairbrush? I could get Kujo to bring Six down to track. He's trained to sniff for bombs, but he might pick up on Molly."

"Do whatever you can," Parker called out, racing for the staircase leading to the first level of the lodge.

He ran down the stairs as fast as he could. Hank and Bastian followed. Colin and Angus found a back staircase and continued to the basement laundry room.

When Parker reached the first floor, he said aloud, "I'm in the front entrance. Which way to the library?"

Swede answered, "Head north. It's below the ballroom."

Parker could hear the sound of the band playing music above. He had a horrible feeling that the lodge was the Titanic with the band playing while the ship sank. He wouldn't let Molly sink with the ship. He hadn't actually told her he loved her. He wanted to say those three words to her face with all the feeling he had in his heart. She was the one for him, damn it.

They'd better not hurt her.

With Swede guiding them down the wide hallway beneath the ballroom, Parker and Hank tried several doors marked "private" or "office". They were locked. When they came to one marked "library", they entered.

Bastian crossed the hallway to a pretty little sitting room with antique sofas and chairs.

Parker and Hank split up, each going a different direction, running their hands along the walls and shelves of books, feeling for levers, buttons or loose books.

"Looks like the passageway might be on the back wall beside a fireplace. Is there a fireplace?"

"Yes." Parker raced for the fireplace. "Which side?"

"The left," Swede said. "Then it travels to the right behind the fireplace and down a set of stairs. Did you find the doorway?"

Parker and Hank studied the wall.

Hank tugged on a shelf. It didn't move or swing open.

Parker gripped a sconce on the wall and tried pulling, twisting and pushing, hoping it was a lever that would release the catch and open the door.

Nothing moved, no door opened, and they stood staring at the wall.

"There has to be something." Parker abandoned the sconce and felt around the bricks of the fireplace. The mortar around one seemed to have chipped away. He touched the brick, and it moved ever so slightly. Parker tried wiggling it and pulling it toward him, but it wouldn't dislodge. Then he leaned into it, pushing hard. The brick slipped forward a few inches, and a click sounded. The bookshelf beside the fireplace shifted.

"It's here," Parker said. He gripped the edge of the shelf and pulled it toward him, revealing the door to the hidden passage. A staircase led downward and turned to the right past the back of the brick fireplace. Just like Swede said. "We're in," Parker said.

"I'm sending you a screenshot of the architectural drawings of the house and the schematics for the mining tunnels in case we lose connection. Some of those secret passages go down deep. Deeper than the basement. They probably connect to the mine at some point."

Parker's phone chirped with an incoming text message with the schematics attached. "Got it." He enlarged the blueprints of the lodge and studied it for a moment.

Hank pointed at the screen. "That's the library." He traced the passage to a level lower than the basement to a series of other passages that crisscrossed. One led downward from the sitting room across the hallway. Another from somewhere in the kitchen.

Parker started into the opening.

"Don't go off half-cocked. Let's get others in place." Hank spoke into his headset. "Bastian, did you find the passageway in the sitting room?"

"Not yet," Bastian's voice sounded in Parker's ear.

"Try the bricks in the fireplace," Hank instructed. "We've got ours open. Need you in yours as we go down."

"There's nothing in the laundry room," Angus reported. "No sign of Molly or the Griffith woman."

"Lewis Griffith is still in the ballroom," Duncan said.

"Boomer, keep an eye on Griffith," Hank ordered. "If he leaves the ballroom, follow him."

"Roger," Boomer responded.

"Kujo," Hank called out. "We could use you and Six on the first floor."

"On my way," the retired dog handler said.

"Angus and Colin," Hank said. "Join Bastian in the sitting room."

Moments later, Bastian reported. "Found the door."

Kujo entered the library with his German Shepherd, Six.

"Ready?" Parker asked. "I've got point."

"Go," Hank said. "Watch for booby traps and bad guys with guns."

Parker led the way downward into the bowels of the lodge, following a narrow passage of wooden stairs that twisted and turned, leading downward. He used his cellphone flashlight to illuminate the way.

When they reached the bottom of the staircase, it opened into a small storage area with shelves against the wall. The shelves were lined with tools and helmets that could be used in mining. At the far end of the room was a heavy iron door.

Angus, Colin, and Bastian arrived a moment later and joined them at the iron door.

Each man drew a gun from beneath the jackets of their suits.

Parker held his ready as he pulled the handle of the iron door.

It creaked open, exposing a dark, long tunnel with railroad tracks leading deep into the mountain.

Parker's breath caught and held. From what Swede had said, and what they'd seen on the schematic of the mine tunnels, there would be many paths.

"They could be anywhere in there," Hank whispered. "Now would be the time for you to come up with something belonging to Molly."

Parker shook his head. "I have nothing."

Hank grinned and held up a small, hand-held tracking device. "That's okay. We have this with a whole lot of blips on it and only one all by itself. It's faded, but I think we can still use it to lead us where we want to go."

"Molly," Parker said dragging air back into his lungs, along with hope. "Let's get going before they do something stupid to Molly or her father."

THE EFFECTS of the drug had already started wearing off by the time Traci Griffith's minions transported her down a secret passageway to the entrance of a mining tunnel. From there, she'd been dumped into a small iron rail bucket and pushed through tunnels, going deeper and deeper into the mountain.

She faded in and out of consciousness. The drug made her so sleepy she couldn't have moved even if she'd wanted to.

When at last they came to a large open area, they brought the rail bucket to a halt and lifted her out. She was plunked onto a wooden chair with arms sitting in the middle of the space. Her wrists were bound to the arms of the chair with duct tape. A single light hung from the ceiling, casting a dull yellow glow around her. Anything outside the circle of light was shrouded in shadow.

Traci Griffith stepped out of the shadows, tapping a pistol in the palm of her hand. Dressed in a beautiful red gown, she was incongruous to the setting, except for the evil glimmer in her eyes.

"Let's get this party started. We don't have a lot of time for this lovely reunion."

"You have no right to detain me," Molly said.

Traci sneered. "Who said I wanted permission? Down here, anything goes, and nobody finds out."

"What have you done with my father?" Molly demanded. She fought to make her voice tough, commanding, but her words slurred, the residual effect of the drug still working its way out of her system.

"Darling," Traci said. "I'm all for family reunions." She looked past Molly toward a couple of the men who'd brought Molly to this hell hole.

The men disappeared into the darkness.

"I wanted to kill you," Traci said, "but I thought about it and realized I needed you alive. The sooner you make your father talk, the sooner I can get out of here and leave the rest of your family alone. You want that, don't you?"

Her voice softened, giving her words a creepily sweet tone that lifted the hairs on Molly's arms.

"You'd hate it if I contracted to kill every member of your family, wouldn't you? All the way down to that sweet little baby of Duncan's."

Anger burned away the dizziness. "You're not even human, torturing an old man and threatening his grandchild."

Traci snorted. "You don't know the lengths I've gone through to get that money. It should have been mine long ago, if that idiot Reed hadn't screwed up and gotten caught. I could have been sitting on a beach, drinking Mai Tais for the past few years. Instead, I'm living in this hellishly cold state, married to another idiot who thinks the lodge is worth saving. The only reason I've stayed as long as I have is because I was told there was a rich vein of gold in here that has yet to be tapped."

She shook her head.

"Well, there isn't. They tapped all the gold veins to be had, and now there isn't even enough dust to buy a beer at that sleazy shit bar in Eagle Rock. I'm done! I was done a few years ago."

Molly shook her head to clear it. "So, you're the one who set up Williams to rob that armored car?"

"You don't think he was smart enough to pull it off on his own, do you? He could barely get himself out of the jail transport when I ran it off the road. I want that money, and I'll start killing off McKinnons, one at a time, until I get it."

Her two goons reappeared out of the darkness,

carrying a bound man dressed in ragged clothing, covered in dried blood and filth. They dropped him on the floor at Molly's feet.

His hair was gray, shaggy and dirty, and his face was bruised and haggard.

Molly recognized him despite his swollen eyes and busted, chapped lips. "Oh, Dad," she cried. "What has this bitch done to you?"

He struggled to sit up. "Molly. Molly girl," he said, his voice rough and sounding old. "You should have stayed away."

"We're going to get you out of here. I swear to you." Her face hardened, and her lips pulled back in a snarl. "And she's going to pay for what she's done to you."

"The only person who's going to get paid is me. Time's up, James," Traci said. She nodded to the man who'd dumped him on the ground. He lifted a small cylinder with a long metal nozzle off the floor, twisted a knob and used an igniter to light the flame.

Molly's heart beat faster. She forced herself to remain calm. "I don't know who you are, mister, but you don't want to do anything with that. Trust me. This woman isn't worth the trouble you'll be in if you kill someone for her. She's not going to pay you anyway."

"Shut up," Traci said. "Do it," she commanded the man with the brazing torch.

Molly spoke low and slow, hoping she sounded

convincing. "If she gets her money, she'll kill you to keep it all for herself. She's greedy. Haven't you learned that by now? She killed William Reed after he stole the money for her. What do you think she'll do to you?"

"Enough!" Traci yelled. She pointed the gun at Molly and turned to Molly's father. "Tell me what Reed told you, or your pretty little girl is going to be burned over every inch of her body."

James McKinnon shook his head. "Please. Don't do this. I've already told you what Reed told me."

"You lie!" Traci screeched. "Tell me where Reed hid the money."

"He said it was hidden where the eagle flies into the mountain. That's what he said. *All* he said, before he died."

"It can't be. It doesn't make sense. Eagles fly all over these damned Crazy Mountains." Traci waved the gun in the air. "He had to have told you exactly where. He said I've had it all along. He lied. You lie. Now your daughter is going to pay for your lies." She waved her gun at the man with the torch. "Burn her."

The man's eyes narrowed. "Is she telling the truth?" the man asked. "Are you going to kill us next?"

"Damn it. I told you she lies. Of course, I'm going to pay you." Her lips pressed into a thin line. "But if you don't burn her now, I'll shoot you and let Dan collect all the money I owe you as well as what I owe him. So, what's it to be?" She aimed her gun at the man with the torch.

The man's eyes narrowed. "Never should've taken this shit job."

"Yeah, well you did, and now you need to do what I'm paying you to do. Burn her."

"No. Please," Molly's father begged. "Please. I told you what I know. I've told you from the beginning."

"Dad, we're going to be okay. She's not going to get away with this. She's going to pay for what she's done to you. To our family."

Traci glared at the man with the torch. "Burn. Her."

Molly's heart ached at the desperation in her father's voice. She hated that he was so worn and damaged, but he was more worried about her than himself.

The cool metal of the necklace around her neck reminded her that she wasn't alone. Help was near. All she had to do was hold out long enough for them to find her.

And help them find her...

As the man approached her with the torch, she looked him in the eye and whispered, "Don't do it."

He hesitated but moved forward, the gun on him a bigger motivator than her eyes begging him not to hurt her.

As the flame neared her skin, she drew in a breath

from deep down in her diaphragm and let loose the loudest scream she could muster.

Her tormentor jerked the flame back, his eyes wide. "I haven't even touched her."

"Then do it, you idiot!" Traci yelled.

Molly sucked in another breath and screamed again. The sound echoed off the walls of the mine.

The whole time, Molly prayed her knight in shining armor, and the cavalry with him, would come riding in to rescue her and her father before it was too late.

CHAPTER 14

PARKER PULLED up the schematic for the mine on his cellphone and cursed the small screen. He needed it to be bigger so he could see quickly and easily where the most likely place they would have taken her was in the mine.

For a few precious minutes, he scrolled through the image looking for what, he didn't know. Then a place on the map appeared that looked like a widening in the tunnels. Several feeders branched out from that wide area. Two of them circled back to where they stood at the entrance of the mine.

"There," he said, pointing to the wide point. "If they have more than one prisoner, plus the people Traci needs to subdue them, wouldn't she take them to a place big enough to hold them?"

"I hope you're right," Angus said.

"I hope I'm right as well." Parker drew in a deep

breath. "If we head the wrong direction, we waste time."

"We can't afford to waste time," Bastian said. "That's my bratty little sister out there, taking one for the team."

"And our father," Angus said.

"Since there are two tunnels leading to this junction, let's split up and meet there." Hank held up the GPS tracker. "I'll know if we're heading in the right direction if the tracker indicates we're getting closer."

"Bastian, Colin and I will take the right tunnel," Angus said. "We might lose communications the deeper we go into the mine. Solid granite walls will cut off signal."

"Then we keep moving forward until we reach the junction," Parker said. "Hold out your cellphone. I'll transfer the schematic to you."

They spent another few seconds sending the schematic over to Angus's cellphone. When he had it and could bring it up on his screen, he held up the device. "Got it."

"Good," Parker said. "Let's go bring Molly and your father home."

With Hank and his GPS tracker behind him, Parker led the way holding his cellphone up as a flashlight, stopping at junctions to check with the old schematic. They followed a narrow rail track into the mine. He prayed he was heading in the right direction and that Molly would be there when they arrived.

"We're getting closer to Molly's tracking device," Hank said. "She's a hundred yards ahead."

Inside the maze of tunnels, a hundred yards might as well have been miles. The deeper they went, the more often Parker had to stop and consult the map. He noticed that at every juncture when he checked the map, they continued along the track.

"That track is leading us to where we're going," Parker whispered.

"Fifty yards," Hank said.

At that moment a blood-curdling scream echoed down the tunnel toward them.

"Molly," Parker said and started running down the track, holding his cellphone high to see where he was placing his feet on the rails and crossbeams.

"Twenty yards," Hank called out loud enough for Parker to hear, but not loud enough to be heard by others.

Another scream ripped through the tunnel, much closer now.

Ahead, the tunnel made a sharp turn to the right. Parker remembered that the widening junction was preceded by just such a jag. He slowed as he neared.

"She's close," Hank whispered. "Angus, we're closing in on the junction. Can you hear me? Where are you?"

"I read you," Angus said. "We're coming up on the junction now. We heard Molly's screams."

Another scream sliced through Parker's heart. "I'm going in."

"We're going in," Hank said into his headset.

"Roger," Angus said.

Parker ran to the curve in the tunnel and shut off his cellphone flashlight when he saw the faint glow of light ahead. He slowed, but continued forward, his gun in his hand.

He could make out the silhouettes of people in the opening ahead. A larger form carrying what appeared to be a brazing torch advanced on a figure seated in a wooden chair.

Molly.

Parker sped up, bursting into the tunnel junction as the man with the torch leaned toward Molly.

"Stop!!!" he yelled. "Hurt her, and I'll make you wish you'd never been born." He held his gun in front of him, aiming at the man holding the torch. "Drop the torch."

"I suggest you drop your gun, or I'll kill your precious girlfriend," a woman's voice sounded from the other side of the big man. Traci stepped into the light coming from a bulb hanging from the ceiling. Her gun was aimed at Molly's head. "Drop it."

Parker held steady. "You drop your gun, and I might let you live."

Traci laughed. "I don't see how you're going to

win this argument when I have the barrel of my gun on her head and my finger on the trigger. Shoot me, I automatically pull the trigger, and your little princess dies."

"Shoot the bitch," Molly said, her voice low and angry. "She doesn't deserve to live after what she's done to my father. Shoot her."

"Shut up," Traci said. "Your family has been nothing but a pain in my ass since this all began. If your father hadn't shown up in that cave when he did, Will would've taken me to the money. I'd have been out of this godforsaken state and country and away from that idiot I married."

"Drop the gun, Traci," Parker warned.

The man holding the brazing torch twisted the knob, turning off the gas to the flame. He set the canister on the ground and backed away from Traci.

"What are you doing?" she asked, her voice rising.

"Like you said...I'm done." He held up his hands.

Traci turned to her other man who held a gun in his hand. "Shoot him."

The man shook his head. "No." Then he held up his hands, bent down and laid his gun on the ground, kicking it across the floor toward Parker. "I'm done, too."

"Cowards. They don't have the upper hand. I'm walking out of this mine with her."

"That will be kind of hard, considering I'm bound to this chair," Molly pointed out. "You'll have to remove this tape first. And to do so, you'll need to put down your weapon." Molly smiled. "Face it, Traci. It's over."

"It's not over until I say it's over," she bit out. With her free hand, she reached into the slit of her skirt and pulled a knife out of a sheath attached to her thigh. She leaned forward, touched the tip of the knife to the tape and ripped it upward and forward, slicing through the layers.

Molly pulled her wrist free.

Traci moved behind Molly, continuing to press the barrel of her weapon against Molly's hair. "I should have killed your father a long time ago. Keeping him alive has been a constant thorn in my side." She leaned over and sliced through the tape on Molly's other wrist.

Molly winced as the blade sliced into her skin but didn't say anything as she pulled her wrist free, blood dripping onto the floor of the mine tunnel.

"You never should have messed with the McKinnons." Molly leaned a little forward and pushed backward as hard as she could, ramming into Traci's belly and knocking her backward.

The gun went off, the bullet ricocheting off the walls.

Parker ducked, rolled to the side and came up running toward Molly and Traci. Molly rolled over onto all fours and jumped onto Traci, pinning her wrist to the ground.

Traci pulled the trigger again, the bullet hitting the mine tunnel, the sound reverberating through the open room.

A loud cracking sounded, like wood splintering, and a subsequent rumbling started slowly.

"Let go of the gun," Molly shouted.

Parker stood over Traci and Molly, pointing his weapon at Traci. "Do as she said. Let go of the gun."

"No way in hell. If I'm going down, you're all coming with me." She fired off several more rounds until the gun clicked empty.

The rumbling grew louder.

Angus burst into the junction. "The brace struts are broken. We have to get out of here. Now!"

"Get Dad," Molly called out. "Get him out of here."

"I'm not going without you, Molly Girl," her father said.

When Traci's two minions took off down the tunnel, Hank let them go. "We'll get them later. Right now, we need all of us to move fast."

Traci laughed. "You're not going to make it. You're all going to die. The braces in this old mine are as old as the mine itself. Once they give, the tunnels will cave in. You're all going to die with me."

"The hell we are." Parker helped Molly to her feet. "Get going. I'll get her out of here."

"As far as I'm concerned. We can leave her here to die."

"No way. She needs to rot in prison for the rest of her days."

Molly nodded. "Yeah. They don't serve Mai Tais there, and you won't see another beach for the rest of your life." She stood and pulled Traci to her feet. "Come on. You're getting out of here to answer for your sins."

"The hell I am." Traci turned and ran toward the opposite end of the room.

Angus stepped in front of her, blocking her path.

She tried to duck around him. He stepped in front of her again, bent like a linebacker and plowed into her belly, throwing her over his shoulder. "Let's go."

Colin and Bastian lifted their father between them and started for the tunnel Parker and Hank had come down.

Molly called out. "Wait. Use the bucket." She pointed to the large metal bucket on the track. "Put him in there and move!"

Dust stirred, and the rumbling grew louder.

Parker turned on the flashlight on his phone, took her hand and raced down the track following the bucket car with Mr. McKinnon in it.

The dust thickened, and rocks shook loose from the ceiling. Before long, his flashlight did little to help them see the tracks in front of him.

He held tight to Molly's hand and used his other hand to follow the tunnel. "Stay on the tracks," he called out. "They lead back to the lodge."

He ran, tripping every so often on the railroad ties. Molly stumbled and fell into him. He pulled her up close and slipped his arm around her. They were moving blind, the dust so thick they could barely breathe.

When they made it back to the mine entrance, Parker didn't know it until he came to the stairs leading upward.

"Everyone make it out?" he said into his headset.

One by one, they checked in.

"Colin and I have Dad in the library," Bastian said.

"I've got Traci," Angus said, sounding winded. "We're halfway up the stairs. And if she doesn't stop kicking, I'm going to push her down them."

"Boomer, Kujo, Six and I are right behind you," Hank said. "Keep moving. The collapse is likely to blow a hole in the lodge. Taz, Duncan, evacuate the building, ASAP."

Parker pushed Molly ahead of him on the stairs. "Go, go, go."

Molly ran as fast as she could, zigzagging up the secret passages, coughing in the dust and blinking back the grit in their eyes.

Finally, they burst through the bookcase door into the library.

Hank, Boomer, Kujo and Six emerged next, diving through the door and closing it behind them.

"Where's Mom?" Molly demanded. "Where's Dad?

I'm not leaving this building until I know they're out and safe."

Parker asked into his communications device. "Status of Mom and Dad McKinnon?"

"This is Duncan, Taz and I got Mom out of the building. We're heading for the parking lot."

"Colin here. Dad's in the parking lot. We're trying to find Mom out here. Oh, wait, we found her."

Parker turned to Molly. "They're outside and safe. "We have to move. Now."

The floor beneath them shook, the rumbling sound building to a roar.

Everyone ran for the hallway.

Parker wrapped his arm around Molly's waist and half lifted her off her feet, moving her as quickly as he could toward the exit.

Behind him, timbers cracked, ceiling panels dropped, and the world came crashing down.

They had just made it out the front entrance when the mountain exploded. The blast of dust and debris shot Parker and Molly forward.

They landed on their knees.

Parker lunged to his feet, scooped Molly into his arms and ran from the fury of the mountain.

When they reached the parking lot, people stood staring at the lodge behind Parker and Molly.

"Put me down," Molly said.

He did, and she ran to where her mother and

father stood holding each other, covered in dust from the blast.

The crowd of people faced the lodge and watched as it seemed to tremble and shake. The roof caved in, taking the walls down around it.

A collective cry went up from the onlookers.

Parker joined Molly beside her parents. She stepped into his embrace and slipped her arms around his waist. "I knew you'd find me," she said.

He chuckled and pulled her closer. "I might not have found you in time, if I hadn't heard your scream."

She grinned, her face caked in dust, her beautiful dress a disaster, and Parker still couldn't think of anyone more beautiful. "By the way, you look beautiful tonight."

She snorted and smoothed a hand over her dusty hair. "I'm a mess."

"A beautiful mess," he said and bent to kiss her dirty lips. "Before anything else happens, because we all know that where Molly goes, trouble follows, I just want to say out loud and for everyone who cares to listen...I love you, Molly McKinnon."

Molly looked up into his face, tears making muddy tracks down her face. "I love you, too, Parker Bailey. And you look amazing in a suit covered in half a mountain. Thank you for saving my life."

"Sweetheart, you were doing a pretty good job on your own." He held her close while the crowd slowly dispersed, driving away from the building they'd come that evening to save.

The sheriff arrived, arresting Traci Griffith and her two minions, who'd voluntarily turned themselves in. The men were willing to tell everything they knew, in exchange for leniency on their sentences.

Mr. Griffith stood in front of the Lucky Lady Lodge, looking like a lost soul. He'd lost his wife to the law, as well as the lodge he'd dedicated his life to since his marriage to Traci.

Parker felt sorry for the man. According to the sheriff, Lewis Griffith hadn't known about his wife's activities. He'd assumed her frequent absences were because she was having an affair.

An ambulance arrived to collect Mr. McKinnon. Mrs. M rode with him to the hospital in Bozeman, where she'd spent the night not long before.

Parker kissed the top of Molly's dusty head. "Are you ready to go home?"

"I am," she said. "Now that the danger is past, Angus will be needing his room back. Unless he decides to stay with Bree indefinitely."

"I guess I'll go back to living in the foreman's cottage."

"Don't you have a king-sized bed in that cottage?"

"I do."

She arched an eyebrow. "Seems a shame to have such a big bed all to yourself."

Parker drew a deep breath. "It is a shame, but it'll have to be that way."

Molly frowned. "What do you mean?"

"Your father's back. Until I get his approval to see his daughter, we'll be sleeping in separate beds."

"The hell, we will." Molly's brow dipped low. "I'm a grown woman. I decide who I sleep with, not my father."

"Maybe your sleeping partner has an equal say regarding that decision."

"Technically speaking, my father isn't back yet. Most likely, he's going to stay at the hospital tonight."

"You have a point," Parker said, narrowing his eyes.

Molly lifted her chin. "Damn right, I do."

"I guess I could bend the rules one more night, just until your father is officially home." He squeezed her gently. "I feel the need for a shower."

"Me, too," Molly said, smiling now.

Parker's pulse quickened. A shower with Molly would be the best thing that had happened to him all day. He was ready. Her father wouldn't be home any earlier than tomorrow, at which time, he'd ask for his permission to date his daughter. Hell, was it too soon for him to cut to the chase and ask Mr. McKinnon if he could marry his daughter?

The thought made his chest swell with all the love he had for this dust-covered beauty standing beside him. He was ready to take on the old Marine for a chance to spend the rest of his life with Molly.

"You two ready to go?" Angus and Bree walked to them from where they'd been talking to the sheriff.

"Yes," Molly said. She was past ready to get out of the dress and the heels that were biting into her feet. She was surprised they'd held together during their mad dash out of the mine and the lodge.

"Mom said not to come to the hospital tonight," Angus said. "She'd call and give us an update on Dad's condition after the ER doctor has a chance to look him over."

They climbed into the dust-covered truck and followed the other cars and trucks out of the parking lot, heading back through Eagle Rock and out to the Iron Horse Ranch.

As they turned in at the gate, Angus slowed to wait for the automatic gate to open. "Looks like what my brothers and I came home to do is done. Our father is safe. Now, we have to make some decisions." He looked down at Bree.

"Sweetheart," she said "if the military is what you want, we can figure it out. I can hire a foreman to run the ranch, and I'll follow you."

"I have a few days to decide before I have to return to duty," he said. "We can discuss it tomorrow. Today was full enough."

Bree reached across the console for his hand and held it all the way up to the house.

Molly slipped her hand into Parker's. She hadn't realized how hard it must have been for her brothers to leave home and join the military. Nor did she understand how hard it was, now, to decide whether to stay in Montana or go back to the military they loved.

If they stayed at the Iron Horse Ranch, her role at the ranch would change. The ranch might not need a foreman. Parker would leave to look for another job.

She squeezed Parker's hand. No matter what the changes were, she'd proven to herself she could handle just about anything. Anything but losing a member of her family. As far as she was concerned, Parker was a member of her family.

She loved him and would stay with him for as long as he let her.

THAT NIGHT, she and Parker took that shower together and made love in his bed until the early hours of the morning.

He held her in his arms as she closed her eyes. "In case I haven't told you enough, I love you."

She chuckled and snuggled up to him. "You've told me at least ten times tonight."

"Not enough?" he asked. "Then let me tell you again. I love you."

She pressed a kiss to his chest. "I love you, too."

"I almost lost you tonight," he said. "I could lose

almost anything, but if I lost you, I would lose my reason for living."

"You had a funny way of showing it for the past five years," she said, tracing the circle around his nipple.

"Trust me, it wasn't easy to keep my hands off you."

"And now?" she asked, her hand slipping down his torso to encircle his hardening shaft.

He rolled her onto her back and leaned over her, his cock nudging her entrance. "Impossible." Then he kissed her and made love to her again.

Molly fell asleep in his arms, happier than she'd ever been, now that everything was right in her world.

EPILOGUE

P ARKER RETURNED to his routine of caring for the ranch and animals, with one change. Instead of avoiding Molly, he worked alongside her, taking every opportunity he could find to kiss her and hold her close.

Mr. McKinnon stayed two nights in the Bozeman hospital while recovering from a few cracked ribs, severe dehydration, and general crankiness. After the second night, the doctors and nurses were more than happy to release him to go home.

Angus and Bree made the trip to Bozeman to bring the older man home.

The entire family, along with their significant others and fiancées, were there to greet him.

"I swear, a man can't go on vacation for a couple of weeks without his children getting into all kinds of trouble," he said as he walked up the steps to the house with the help of Angus on one side and his wife on the other.

"I've had a chance to meet Bree, and I couldn't be happier for Angus. About time you found someone to settle down with. I'm glad to hear you'll be coming home for good when your enlistment is up. Between Bree's place and the Iron Horse Ranch, you'll be busy."

Mr. McKinnon turned to Colin and Emily. "Hi, Emily. I remember you from when you, Colin and Alex used to ride all over the ranch together as teens. I'm glad you're going to be part of our family. Are you sure you want to follow this Marine around the world?"

Emily nodded. "I'm up for a little adventure."

"And a good thing. It's not easy being a military wife."

She squared her shoulders. "I can handle it, as long as I have Colin."

The older McKinnon turned to Jenna who stood beside Bastian. "I hear you were the one who discovered the abandoned house where Otis Ferguson treated me to some of his kind of fun." His lips pressed together. "I'm glad you and Bastian got him. I'm even happier Bastian found someone to love. How do you feel about living on the Iron Horse Ranch?"

"I already am," she said with a smile. "And I love it."

"Hannah," Mr. McKinnon shot a smile at his wife. "It looks like we need to add some more rooms to the house."

When he came to Duncan, his smile broadened at the baby girl in his arms. "I can't believe I've been gone only a few weeks, and you made me a grandfather." He turned to Fiona and took her hand in both of his. "Thank you."

She brushed a tear from her cheek. "I love your son with all my heart."

"And it's obvious he loves you, too. You two will be busy as we make this ranch even more productive than it is now."

He squeezed her hand, let go and reached for his wife's hand. "Sounds sappy from an old Marine, but love is everything. Without it, I would not have survived as long as I did. It was the thought of seeing my Hannah and my children again that kept me going."

Parker watched Molly as her father made his rounds of each of his sons and their fiancées, accepting them and voicing his approval for his sons' happiness.

Molly and Parker stood back from the rest of the family.

When Molly's father didn't immediately seek her out, Parker slipped his arm around her waist and pulled her close.

She leaned against his side and smiled up at him. "It's okay."

He knew what she meant. Her father had always looked over her to his sons' accomplishments.

As far as Parker was concerned it was not okay. "No. It's not."

He opened his mouth to say something to Mr. McKinnon, when the older man frowned and called out, "Molly Girl? Where are you?"

"I'm here, Dad," she said, stepping forward.

Her father opened his arms. "Come here."

She left Parker's side and stepped into her father's embrace.

"Molly Girl, I wouldn't be here if it weren't for you. When my boys all went off to join the military, you stayed by my side and worked so hard to make up for the fact they were gone. You may think I didn't notice, but I did. I'm so very proud of you and everything you've accomplished here." He smiled over her head at her mother. "Your mother tells me I don't give credit where credit is due. So, I'm giving you credit." He winked down at her. "We couldn't have run this ranch without you."

Parker nodded his head in silence.

"When I hired young Bailey, I thought I was giving you a break to get on with your own life. I wanted you to get off the ranch, date, fall in love, meet someone. I didn't realize you thought I didn't think you could handle the job." He smoothed a hand over her hair. "I'd fire Bailey today, if I thought it would make up for my man-thinking."

"Don't fire him, Daddy," Molly said. "He's good at what he does."

"I know. And I can't fire him, now, because he needs the work to support his family. Or am I wrong about the two of you?" He frowned, looking straight at Parker.

Parker straightened his shoulders. "Sir, you're not wrong about us. I love your daughter." He stepped forward and held out his hand.

Molly placed hers in his.

"And I want to marry her, with your approval."

Molly's father cocked an eyebrow. "I don't know what my approval has to do with anything." He lifted his chin at Molly. "Do you love him?"

She nodded. "Yes, Daddy."

"Do you want to marry him?" her father asked.

She smiled up at Parker. "Yes, Daddy."

"Then you have all the approval you need."

"Thank you, sir. But you kind of stole my moment." Parker grinned. "Seeing as you've already said yes..." he pulled a ring out of his pocket and dropped to one knee. "I think it bears repeating... Molly McKinnon, will you marry me?"

Tears filled Molly's eyes as she drew Parker back to his feet. "Yes. I will marry you. I thought you'd never ask."

"Wait... What's this?" he asked, brushing a tear

from her cheek. "I thought McKinnons never cried."

Molly laughed. "According to my father, we don't."

"Well then, I just broke that rule," her father said gruffly, brushing a tear from his own bruised cheek.

Several vehicles pulled up to the house in time to save them all from more tears.

Hank Patterson, his pregnant wife Sadie and their daughter Emma got out of the first vehicle.

Boomer, his wife Daphne and their daughter Maya got out of the second truck.

"I hope you all don't mind. I invited Hank and his entire team out to the ranch for a cookout," Mr. McKinnon said. "I felt like it was time to celebrate."

"Are you sure you're up to it?" Molly asked.

"Believe me. I'm up to it. They pumped me so full of fluids and vitamins, I'm feeling better already."

Hank came up the steps with Sadie. "The rest of my team is on the way. I wanted to get here early to let you know I followed up on what Parker and Molly told me about what William Reed said about the money being hidden where the eagle flies into the mountain." Hank smiled at Parker and Molly. "You were right. Reed hid the money at that closed mine entrance on the back side of the mountain. We sent a couple of guys up there with shovels and picks and found the bags of money buried beneath the old mine entrance with the flying eagle carved into the entrance timbers."

Molly laughed and hugged Parker.

"That's not all," Hank said. "There was a reward for the return of that money. You two will receive fifty thousand dollars for providing the information that led to the recovery of the money. Congratulations."

"What are you going to do with all that money?" Bastian asked.

Molly looked up at Parker. "What *are* we going to do with it?"

"I know of a lodge that needs a little work. I think we can get it for a song," he said with a crooked grin.

"Actually, I love the idea."

"You'd give up ranching?"

"No. But with all the help we'll have around here, I'll have more time to do other things."

"Like giving me more grandchildren?" her father asked.

Molly's cheeks turned a bright pink. "Dad, we're just barely engaged."

"So?" Her father gave her a cocky grin. "Duncan isn't married yet, and he's already given me a granddaughter. Caity needs cousins."

"We'll get right on that wedding planning," Parker said.

"Good." Molly's father clapped his hands together. "Now, let's get down to the business of celebrating with family and friends."

"You're going to sit and watch while the rest of us celebrate," Mrs. M said.

"But I'm home, and there's grilling to do," her husband protested.

"Not for you," she said. "Sit."

"Yes, ma'am," he said and caught her in a gentle embrace. "I love you, Hannah McKinnon. Thanks for not giving up on me."

"I love you, too, James." She kissed him soundly and pointed to a rocking chair. "Now, do as I said."

Parker pulled Molly to the side and into his arms. "I had a much more romantic setting in mind for asking you to marry me."

Molly looked at the ring on her finger and shook her head. "Your proposal was perfect. You know how much I love my family, and you did it in front of all of them. It was nice to share my joy with all of the people I love. Especially you."

She wrapped her arms around his neck and kissed him long and hard.

Parker held her close, happier than he'd been in a long time. He had Molly, he'd been accepted into her family and he had a future ahead of him full of adventure and love.

He couldn't ask for a happier beginning.

THE END

SEAL JUSTICE

BROTHERHOOD PROTECTORS BOOK #13

New York Times & *USA Today*
Bestselling Author

ELLE JAMES

SEAL JUSTICE

BROTHERHOOD PROTECTORS

New York Times & USA Today Bestselling Author
ELLE JAMES

CHAPTER 1

REGGIE MCDONALD HELD her breath and listened for him. She shivered, her naked body chilled by the cool damp air of her prison. Though her brain was murky, her thoughts unclear, and her strength diminished, she knew what she had to do. When she could hear no sounds of boots on the wooden steps leading down into the earthen cellar, she continued digging. Inch by inch, she scraped away at the soil of her cell, praying she was correct in assuming hers was on the edge of the group of cells. If she dug long enough, she might see daylight and find a way to escape the hell she'd been trapped in for what felt like a lifetime.

Using the tin cup she'd been given to drink from, she scooped dirt from the corner behind the door. That small space was hidden from her captor when he came to feed her or shackle her to take her up to the big house where he tortured her and the other young women he'd kidnapped and held in the horrible dungeon beneath his house.

If she got out, she'd find help to get the other women out and save them from the sociopath who forced them to bow to his bidding. If they didn't do what he said, he whipped them with a riding crop or shocked them with a cattle prod. Sometimes, he burned them with the lit end of the cigars he smoked.

To keep them pliant to his will, he drugged their food and water, making them weak and groggy, unable to form clear thoughts or fight back.

Reggie had caught on to what he'd been doing. She couldn't quit eating or drinking completely, but she'd skip a day and use that time of semi-clear thinking to work through the problem to come up with a solution. On those clear days, she'd acted just as drugged when she'd been shackled and taken up the wooden stairs to the Master's house. When she could see out a window, she'd determined the house sat on the side of a hill, the slope dipping downward from the back of the structure. Though the women were trapped in the cellar, the earthen walls of their prison couldn't be that thick, especially on the far end where she was being kept. The hill sloped sharply on that end, giving her hope that, with steady digging, she'd eventually break free of captivity and escape.

Reggie prayed she was correct and scooped faster, pushing the soil she'd dislodged into the sides of the walls and floor, packing it down so that her captor couldn't tell it was fresh dirt.

She paused again as a sound penetrated the wooden door of her cell.

Footsteps.

"He's coming," a voice whispered. Reggie recognized Terri's voice. She was in the first cell, closest to the stairs. She'd been there the longest. A single mother of a little girl, she'd held out all those days, suffering through the torture in hope of seeing her little girl again. Lately, she'd fallen into despair of ever escaping.

Quiet sobs sounded from other cells along the row.

Reggie emptied her cup, quickly patted the dirt she'd removed into the ground, dragged her tattered blanket over her naked body and moved to the opposite corner where she curled up and pretended to be asleep.

Boots clunked down the steps to the bottom.

Silence reigned, even the few sobs ceased as the women held their breath, praying the Master wouldn't choose them for the trip up the stairs.

Reggie waited, listening. When a door hinge creaked, she braced herself.

"Please, no. Please," a woman's voice pleaded with the Master. It was Beth, a young college student who'd been captured on her way home from a night class. "Don't hurt me," she cried.

"Shut up and move," the Master's harsh voice echoed in the darkness.

"No, please. I can't." The sharp crackle of electricity sparking was followed by a scream.

Reggie winced and bit down hard on her tongue to keep from yelling at the man for hurting Beth. She couldn't draw attention to herself. Not now. Not when the hole she'd been digging was already two feet wide and as deep. If he took Beth up to the house, he'd be distracted long enough Reggie might finally break through.

Beth cried as she stumbled up the stairs, the Master's footsteps sounding as he climbed up behind her.

As soon as the door clicked closed at the top of the stairs, Reggie grabbed her cup and went back to work, digging furiously, scraping the dirt away with the cup and her fingernails. The Master usually kept a woman up in the big house for at least an hour before he brought her back to her cell. She didn't have much time.

She abandoned quiet for speed and dug as fast as she could.

"What are you doing?" Terri whispered, her voice barely carrying above the scraping sound of the cup on dirt and rocks.

Reggie ignored her, determined to get as far as she could before the Master returned.

Her cup struck a large rock. Undeterred, she

scraped around the edges, her heart beating faster, her breath coming in ragged gasps. The drugs in her body slowed her down, making her want to crawl into her blanket and sleep. But she couldn't.

"Stop whatever you're doing," Terri said.

Reggie halted and listened. When she didn't hear footsteps or the quiet sobs of Beth being returned to her cell, she went back to work on digging around the rock.

Soon, she found the edge of one end of the stone and worked her way around it.

After scraping and digging for what felt like an hour, she poked through the dirt and felt cool, fresh air streaming through a tiny hole onto her fingertips.

Not trusting her hands, she pushed her head through the tunnel and sniffed fresh air, the scent of decaying foliage a welcome scent from the earthen cell. She inhaled deeply, her breath catching on a sob. She'd been right. Her cell was on the edge of the hill. If she dug a little more, she might be able to push through. The large rock was in the way. If only…

She pulled her head out of the tunnel and shoved her bare feet in and pushed as hard as she could.

The rock didn't move.

Lying on her back, the cool dirt floor making her shiver, she scooted closer, bunched her legs and kicked hard with her heels, over and over until the rock moved. Hope blossomed in her chest and gave her the strength to keep pushing and kicking.

"You have to stop," Terri said. "When one of us crosses him, he punishes us all."

Another one of the women sobbed. "Please don't make him mad."

Reggie didn't want any of them to be hurt by her actions, but the Master was hurting them every time he took one of them up into the house. She had to get out and get help for all of them. Using every last bit of her strength to kick and shove at the boulder until it rocked and gave, she finally pushed it free of the soil, and it rolled down the hill. Loose dirt fell into the tunnel, blocking the sweet scent of fresh air.

Using her feet again, Reggie pushed at the dirt. More fell into the gap. She scrambled around and shoved her arms through the tight tunnel and patted the loose dirt against the walls of the tunnel, shoving the excess out and down the hill.

"Shh!" Someone said from one of the other cells. "He's coming."

A door opened above them. Sobs sounded as Beth descended into her prison, followed by the clumping sound of the Master's boots.

Reggie hadn't taken the time to pat the dirt into the walls this time. If the Master came into her cell, he'd catch her at digging her way out. She looked through the hole. Gray beckoned her. She shoved her shoulders through the tunnel. It was tight. Really tight. But if she could get her shoulders through, she could get the rest of her body through. Desperately inching and wiggling her way inside, she prayed she could breach the exit before the Master jerked open her door, grabbed her by the ankles and yanked her back inside. He'd beat her and chain her. And he'd throw her into the wooden box beneath the stairs where he kept the "naughty" girls.

No way. She couldn't let that happen. Not when she could taste freedom.

With her body blocking the tunnel, sounds of weeping and cries were muffled. Reggie couldn't tell if the women were informing the Master of her scratching and digging. She wasn't sticking around to find out. Once her shoulders were free, she braced her hands on the edges of the hole and pushed as hard as she could. Her body scraped through until her hips were free of the tunnel. Grabbing onto nearby branches, she pulled her legs out of the hole. Once all of her was free, gravity took hold, and she tumbled down the hill, her skin torn and gouged by sticks, rocks and bramble.

The jabs and tears made her cry out with joy. The pain wasn't inflicted by the Master but delivered by nature as a testament she was out of that hell.

She came to a stop when her head hit the big rock she'd pushed free of her tunnel. For a long moment, she lay still, her vision blurring, pain raking through the base of her skull.

Then she heard the sounds of dogs barking, and her heart froze. The Master had two vicious looking

Rottweilers he'd kept tethered when he'd brought her up into the big house.

Reggie staggered to her bare feet and shivered. The cool night air wrapped around her naked body. Swallowing the sobs rising up her throat, she ran, following the hill downward. She didn't know where she was or which way to go, only that she had to get as far away from the house and the dogs as possible. She hadn't come this far to be ripped apart by his maniacal dogs or dragged back to house and beaten until she couldn't remember who she was or why she cared.

Sticks and rocks dug into the soft pads of her feet, drawing blood. She kept running until her feet were as numb as her skin and mind. The dogs were getting closer. She had to do something to lose them.

The hill continued downward. A cloud crossed over the sky, blocking what little starlight penetrated the tree branches. Her lungs burning and her heart beating so fast she thought it might explode out of her chest, Reggie was forced to stop long enough for the cloud to shift, allowing the starlight to illuminate her way.

When it did, she stared out at a dark canyon. She stood on the edge of a precipice. Easing to the edge, she could see the glint of starlight off what appeared to be a river forty feet below where she stood.

The barking dogs were close now.

Reggie turned right then left. No matter which

way she went, the cliffs were still as high as the one in front of her. She couldn't backtrack. The dogs were so close enough, they'd find her.

She refused to give up. But what else could she do? Die from the vicious rendering of sharp Rottweiler teeth, go back willingly to the Master's house to be beaten, or jump off a cliff into water of which she had no idea of the depth?

When the barking sounded right behind her, Reggie spun to face the two Rottweilers, emerging from the tree line...stalking her.

A shout from behind them made her heart leap into her throat. The Master.

Without further thought or mental debate, Reggie turned and threw herself over the cliff.

As she plunged downward, she steeled herself for the impact against rocks or whatever lay beneath the water's surface.

Crossing her arms over her chest, pointed her toes and hit the river feet-first, sinking deep. The chill shocked her body, but she kept her mouth shut tight, and struggled, kicking hard to rise. Just when she thought she would never breathe again, she bobbed to the surface and gasped. Above her, she heard the wild barking of the Rottweilers.

The cold water helped clear her foggy brain. She had to make the Master think she was dead. Taking a deep breath, she lay over, face-first in the water and floated as far as she could before turning her head to the side to take another breath. She did this for as long as she could hear the dogs barking above. The Master had to think she'd died in the fall from the cliff. It was the only way to get away and make him think she couldn't tell the authorities about what he had hidden in his basement.

After a while, the sound of the dogs barking faded. Knowing the dogs couldn't follow her scent in the water, she let the river's current carry her along as she treaded water to keep her head above the surface.

The cold sapped what little energy she had left. She rolled onto her back and floated into the shallows where she dragged herself up onto the shore.

Darkness surrounded her, embraced her and sucked her under. As she faded into unconsciousness, her last thought was...*I'm free.*

ABOUT THE AUTHOR

ELLE JAMES also writing as MYLA JACKSON is a *New York Times* and *USA Today* Bestselling author of books including cowboys, intrigues and paranormal adventures that keep her readers on the edges of their seats. When she's not at her computer, she's traveling, snow skiing, boating, or riding her ATV, dreaming up new stories. Learn more about Elle James at www.ellejames.com

Website | Facebook | Twitter | GoodReads | Newsletter | BookBub | Amazon

Or visit her alter ego Myla Jackson at mylajackson.com
Website | Facebook | Twitter | Newsletter

Follow Me!
www.ellejames.com
`ellejames@ellejames.com

ALSO BY ELLE JAMES

Navy SEAL Survival

Navy SEAL Captive

Navy SEAL To Die For

Navy SEAL Six Pack

Devil's Shroud Series

Deadly Reckoning (#1)

Deadly Engagement (#2)

Deadly Liaisons (#3)

Deadly Allure (#4)

Deadly Obsession (#5)

Deadly Fall (#6)

Covert Cowboys Inc Series

Triggered (#1)

Taking Aim (#2)

Bodyguard Under Fire (#3)

Cowboy Resurrected (#4)

Navy SEAL Justice (#5)

Navy SEAL Newlywed (#6)

High Country Hideout (#7)

Clandestine Christmas (#8)

Thunder Horse Series

Hostage to Thunder Horse (#1)

Thunder Horse Heritage (#2)

Thunder Horse Redemption (#3)

Christmas at Thunder Horse Ranch (#4)

Demon Series

Hot Demon Nights (#1)

Demon's Embrace (#2)

Tempting the Demon (#3)

Lords of the Underworld

Witch's Initiation (#1)

Witch's Seduction (#2)

The Witch's Desire (#3)

Possessing the Witch (#4)

Stealth Operations Specialists (SOS)

Nick of Time

Alaskan Fantasy

Blown Away

Stranded

Feel the Heat

The Heart of a Cowboy

Protecting His Heroine

Warrior's Conquest

Rogues

Enslaved by the Viking Short Story

Conquests

Smokin' Hot Firemen

Love on the Rocks

Protecting the Colton Bride

Protecting the Colton Bride & Colton's Cowboy Code

Heir to Murder

Secret Service Rescue

High Octane Heroes

Haunted

Engaged with the Boss

Cowboy Brigade

Time Raiders: The Whisper

Bundle of Trouble

Killer Body

Operation XOXO

An Unexpected Clue

Baby Bling

Under Suspicion, With Child

Texas-Size Secrets

Cowboy Sanctuary

Lakota Baby

Dakota Meltdown

Beneath the Texas Moon